mary-kateandashley

so little time

Check out these other great

so little time

titles:

Book 1: **how to train a boy**

Book 2: **instant boyfriend**

Book 3: **too good to be true**

Book 4: **just between us**

Book 5: **tell me about it**

Book 6: **secret crush**

Book 7: **girl talk**

Book 8: **the love factor**

Book 9: **dating game**

Book 10: **a girl's guide to guys**

Book 11: **boy crazy**

Book 12: **best friends forever**

Coming soon!

Book 14: **spring breakup**

mary-kateandashley

so little time

love is in the air

By Eliza Willard

Based on the series Created by Eric Cohen
and Tonya Hurley

HarperCollins*Entertainment*
An Imprint of HarperCollins*Publishers*

A PARACHUTE PRESS BOOK

A PARACHUTE PRESS BOOK

Parachute Publishing, L.L.C.
156 Fifth Avenue
Suite 302
NEW YORK
NY 10010

First published in the USA by HarperEntertainment 2004
First published in Great Britain by HarperCollins*Entertainment* 2005
HarperCollins*Entertainment* is an imprint of HarperCollins*Publishers* Ltd,
77-85 Fulham Palace Road, Hammersmith, London W6 8JB

The HarperCollins website address is
www.harpercollins.co.uk

2

ISBN 0 00 718094 2

Printed and bound in Great Britain by Clays Ltd, St Ives plc

chapter one

"Three days until V-Day!" fourteen-year-old Chloe Carlson said, feeling all warm and fuzzy inside. "Valentine's Day!"

"You mean, three days until D-Day," her twin sister, Riley, said. "Doomsday."

It was Tuesday morning. Chloe, Riley, and their friend Tara Jordan were hanging in the girls' bathroom on the second floor at school, waiting for Sierra Pomeroy to finish changing her clothes.

[Chloe: Let me explain. It's not that Sierra couldn't decide what to wear this morning and brought another option. It's that her parents make her wear boring, conservative clothes all the time. So every morning Sierra changes her outfit as soon as she gets to school. Her parents have no idea. In fact, there's a lot her parents don't know – like how she changed her name from Sarah to

Sierra, like how she plays bass guitar in a rock band called The Wave, like how she sort of lives a double life....]

"How can you say that, Riley?" Sierra asked, emerging from a stall wearing a black suede miniskirt and a black T-shirt. She undid her ponytail and started fluffing her wavy red hair to make it look bigger. "Don't you have a date with that guy Andrew after school today?"

"Yes," Riley admitted.

"So maybe it will be great!" Sierra went on. "Maybe you'll go totally crazy over him! Maybe he'll even be your valentine!"

"Yeah, maybe," Riley said. "But I'm not getting my hopes up."

"Why not?" Tara asked.

[Chloe: I was there when Riley met Andrew. It was at Quinn Reyes's party last weekend. We don't know him very well because he goes to Beverly Hills High. But I watched them from across the room. Andrew was really into Riley – I could tell from his body language.]

"Yeah, what's the problem, Riley?" Chloe asked, checking her lip gloss in the mirror. "Andrew is really cute. How bad could it be?"

"Oh, it could be bad," Riley said. "Reality check? Do I have to remind you that bad dates exist? Even the cutest guys can have zero personality. Remember Cory? Last week?"

"Oh, yeah," Chloe said, remembering. "You didn't have such a great time with him."

"To put it mildly," Riley said.

[Chloe: Cory is a sophomore. He asked Riley to spend an afternoon on the beach with him. She thought it was a date, but I'm not so sure he did.]

"He seemed nice and everything," Riley explained to Sierra and Tara. "But then, while we were walking on the beach, we ran into his friends. He invited them all to come hang out with us!"

"Ouch," Sierra said.

"From then on he basically ignored me," Riley said. "Our 'date' was pretty much Cory and his friends playing touch football on the beach while I sat alone and watched. They wouldn't even let me play!"

"That *was* pretty bad," Chloe admitted. "Oh! And there was that guy who never stopped calling you. Remember? He'd call you the day before the date and say, 'Don't forget about our date tomorrow!' Then he'd call you the morning of the date, half an hour before he picked you up, right after he dropped you off, an hour later, the next morning. . . ."

"So you can see why I'm not all that excited about my date tonight with Andrew," Riley said, "or for Valentine's Day."

"Well, I say give Andrew a chance anyway. You never know when the right guy will come along," Chloe said, thinking about her boyfriend, Lennon Porter. "As for me, I can't wait for Valentine's Day!"

[Chloe: This is my first Valentine's Day with a real boyfriend! That's why I'm acting like such a goof about it. I'm usually much cooler than this – really!]

"How are you and Lennon going to celebrate?" Tara asked.

"I'm not sure," Chloe said. "We haven't talked about it yet."

"Do you think he'll give you a present?" Tara asked.

"Probably," Sierra said. "Isn't that what boys are supposed to do on Valentine's Day?"

Chloe felt that gushy feeling come over her again. "I wonder what he'll give me," she said. "A big heart-shaped box of chocolates? Flowers? A beautiful card?"

Or something even more special? Chloe wondered. Something that shows how he feels about me? Like maybe jewelry or a poem he wrote himself?

She was too embarrassed to talk about that with her friends or even with Riley. But deep down she was hoping for something really romantic from Lennon. Something just between the two of them that no one else would share. The ultimate gooey valentine! She had to think of something really good to give him, too.

"We'll see," Riley warned. "Boys can be totally clueless about that stuff sometimes."

"I have a feeling Lennon will come through," Chloe said with a smile. "You guys, this is going to be my first real romantic-y boyfriend-y Valentine's Day! I am so psyched!" she added, sort of bouncing on her toes.

Tara laughed. "I can't believe what a goofball you are! You'd think it was first grade and you'd gotten the most valentines in the class."

"I do feel like that," Chloe admitted, "only better!"

The girls laughed, and Riley shook her head. "I guess that's what love does to people," she said.

The bell rang – it was time for homeroom. "Want to meet in the courtyard before third period?" Chloe asked as the girls gathered their things together.

"Definitely," Riley agreed.

"See you there," Tara said.

Chloe picked up her books and made her way down the crowded hallway toward her homeroom. She spotted Lennon up ahead, talking to his friends Zach Block and Sebastian Lee. Lennon's locker was open, and he stood on the other side of it, half-hidden by the door. But Chloe recognized him by his sneakers and the way he moved his hands a lot when he talked.

I'll just say a quick hello, Chloe thought as she moved closer. But she couldn't help overhearing what the boys were saying.

"So it's this Friday, three days away," Lennon said. "It's going to be so cool! But it's top secret, okay? I totally want to surprise Chloe."

Sebastian and Zach nodded.

"No problem," Zach said.

A surprise? On Friday? Chloe thought. Awesome! I *knew* he was going to do something romantic for Valentine's Day!

Then Sebastian looked up and saw her. "Hi, Chloe," he said.

Lennon slammed his locker shut and turned to face her.

Chloe couldn't help melting at the sight of him. He was so cute! Tall and lanky with intelligent blue eyes and shaggy brown hair just *this close* to needing a haircut.

"Hey," he said, smiling at her. Then he sort of glanced at the others, as if to say "Don't tell!"

"What's going on?" Chloe asked, acting as if she didn't know a thing.

"Nothing special," Lennon said. "Ready for gym today? Do-si-do!" He grabbed Chloe by the crook of her elbow and swung her around.

Chloe laughed as they did a little dance together. "We have square dancing in gym this week," she explained to Zach and Sebastian as she spun past them.

"Chloe's my partner," Lennon added. "She does a mean promenade!" He switched arms and swung her around again.

Chloe laughed again. She liked the fact that Lennon didn't feel the need to act supercool in front of his friends.

The second bell rang. Lennon gave Chloe a kiss on the cheek. "We'd better get to class," he said. "See you at the hoe-down!"

Chloe hugged her books to her chest as she hurried down the hall. She was so excited, she thought she'd explode!

Lennon was planning a surprise for her – for Valentine's Day! That was so sweet!

But Chloe could hardly stand the suspense. What could the surprise be?

chapter two

"What are you doing for Valentine's Day, Manuelo?" Riley asked after school that afternoon. She was searching through a cupboard in the kitchen, looking for doggie treats for Pepper, the Carlsons' white and brown cocker spaniel.

The puppy barked and sniffed eagerly at her heels.

"Yeah, Manuelo," Chloe added. "Do you have a date?"

"I have no date," Manuelo replied. Manuelo Del Valle was the Carlsons' housekeeper, cook and friend. He'd been with them since Chloe and Riley were babies. "But I don't care!" he added. "I love Valentine's Day. I'm my own best valentine!" He dropped some red food coloring into a bowl of white frosting and stirred it.

Riley's mom and dad were separated, and they were both out of town for the week. Their mom, Macy, was at a fashion convention in New York City. And their dad, Jake, was at a yoga retreat in Sausalito, California. Their parents weren't away at the same time very often, and it was nice to have Manuelo to come home to.

"I'm with you, Manuelo," Riley said, still looking for the dog treats. "Valentine's Day is overrated."

"No! That's not what I'm saying at all," Manuelo said. He started frosting a plate of cupcakes with the pink icing. "Valentine's Day is fabulous! Having a *date* is overrated."

"I bet you'll change your tune after your date with Andrew tonight," Chloe said to Riley. "You'll come home saying 'Will he be my valentine?'"

"Hey, you never know," Riley said. "Aha! Here they are!" She pulled a box of dog treats out of the cupboard and sat on the floor to feed Pepper.

"Who's Andrew?" Manuelo asked.

"This boy I met at Quinn's party last weekend," Riley explained. "He goes to Beverly Hills High."

"He's very cute, Manuelo," Chloe added. "Medium height – just right for Riley. He's got straight brown hair, not too long. He's hot – and smart!"

"He's a sportswriter for his school newspaper," Riley said.

"So what's the matter?" Manuelo asked. "Don't you think you'll have a good time with him?"

Riley shrugged. "I don't know. Lately every time I get near a boy, it ends in disaster. And even if it doesn't..." She sighed. "It just doesn't *click*, you know?"

She couldn't help envying Chloe a little bit. Chloe was so excited about Valentine's Day, and she had such a good thing with Lennon. Riley wanted something like they had. Something special.

"You're just going through a dry spell," Manuelo said, nodding. "It happens. But they don't last forever. And the best way to get through them is to treat yourself to something nice! For Valentine's Day I'm going to buy myself candy and send myself a dozen roses! Red ones – the best kind!"

"I like pink flowers," Riley said. "They remind me of sugar roses on a birthday cake."

"Sure, pink is nice," Manuelo said, "but the best roses to get are red. When someone sends you roses, the color is very important. You send pink roses when someone has done you a favor and you want to thank them. You send white roses to someone you've shared a secret with, or maybe when you have a secret to tell them. Yellow roses mean friendship, and red roses stand for love. If a boy you love sends you a yellow rose, that's not good. It means he only thinks of you as a friend."

"Wow, Manuelo," Chloe said. "I had no idea there was a whole language of roses."

"Sure," Manuelo said. "That's why I only send myself red. Because I love myself!"

Riley's head was suddenly so full of roses – red, pink, white, yellow – she could almost smell them.

"You know, you're right, Chloe," she said. "Maybe this date *will* turn out to be fun. Why shouldn't it? Andrew's cute, and he seems very nice."

"That's the spirit!" Chloe said.

Riley glanced at the clock and jumped up from the floor. "I'd better go change. Andrew is going to be here in half an hour!"

She went to her room and picked out a denim skirt and cute rose-printed top. As she dressed, she started to get excited about her date. Maybe Andrew would break her dry spell. Maybe he'd turn out to be a really cool guy. Maybe she'd have a wonderful time on the date tonight!

The doorbell rang. A few moments later Manuelo called Riley downstairs.

Andrew smiled when he saw her. "You look great."

"Thanks," Riley said. So far, so good, she thought.

They went to the mall to catch an early movie. "What do you want to see?" Andrew asked.

"Well, I've already seen *Space Heroes*, *Power-Mad*, and *The Horse Diaries*," Riley said. "So that just leaves *London Blues* and *Dempsey Strikes Out*."

"Let's see *Dempsey Strikes Out*," Andrew suggested. "I've heard it's great."

"Okay," Riley agreed. All she knew about *Dempsey* was that it was about baseball, and she wasn't that into baseball. But maybe the movie would be good anyway.

Andrew bought them popcorn and drinks, and they settled into their seats. The coming attractions started.

"All right!" Andrew said. "I love to see what movies are on deck for the summer."

"Me, too," Riley said.

Soon the feature started.

It wasn't good. Her first clue that she wouldn't like it came during the opening scene – a baseball game. Most of the movie took place during a baseball game.Dempsey, the main character, had a girlfriend, but all she did was sit in the stands and cheer for him. When Dempsey's team won the World Series at the end, the girlfriend ran out onto the field and hugged him, even though he'd pretty much ignored her through the whole movie.

"What did you think?" Andrew asked when they left the theater.

"Um, it was okay," Riley said. "I probably would have liked it better if it didn't have so much baseball in it, though."

"Really?" Andrew said. "I love baseball movies. But this wasn't my favorite. I thought it hit a double but got thrown out at third."

Riley stared at him. "What are you talking about?"

"You know – it was good at the beginning, but by the end it went downhill."

"Oh." Riley had never heard anyone describe a movie that way before. It was a little weird. But she figured it made sense, in a way, since he was talking about a baseball movie.

"Are you hungry?" Andrew asked. "Maybe you'd like some hot dogs? Peanuts? Cracker Jack?"

Riley laughed. "I get it. You eat that stuff at baseball games, right? How about pizza?" she suggested.

"Good call," Andrew said. "We can get any kind you want – as long as it's pepperoni."

Riley laughed again. "I love pepperoni," she said. "Let's get it."

He's kind of funny, she thought. That was definitely a good thing.

They headed for a pizza place in the mall and ordered a pepperoni pie.

"Sorry. We're out of pepperoni," the girl behind the counter said.

"Out of pepperoni?" Andrew cried. "How can that be? This is a pizza place, isn't it? You can't be out of pepperoni!"

"Yeah, well, we are," the girl said.

Andrew looked at Riley. "But my friend here likes pepperoni."

"It's okay, Andrew. Why don't we just get plain cheese?" Riley suggested. She wasn't sure if he was kidding about the pepperoni or not. "Or any other kind you like. You must like another kind of pizza."

"I guess we'll have cheese," Andrew said.

What was the big deal? Riley wondered. Was he teasing the counter girl by pretending to be upset that they didn't have pepperoni? Or was he really upset?

[Riley: Okay, I know that Andrew is funny, but the question is, is he funny ha-ha? Or funny weird?]

They took their sodas to a table to wait for the pizza.

"That girl really threw me a curve ball," Andrew said, sipping his root beer. "I mean, who ever heard of a pizza place that was out of pepperoni?"

Riley shrugged. "I guess it happens," she said. What's with all the baseball talk? she wondered. *Curve ball? On deck? Thown out at third?*

She fidgeted in her seat. Don't be too judgmental, she told herself. So the guy talks a little funny. Give him a chance. Maybe it's part of his sense of humor.

The pizza came at last. Riley and Andrew dug in.

"So what kinds of things do you like to do?" Riley asked. "Besides cover sports for your school paper?"

"I'm vice president of the student senate," Andrew replied. "I love to run for office. So far I've won every election I've ever entered. I'm batting a thousand! I was president of my junior high, class president every year since fifth grade...."

Riley plastered a smile onto her face and nodded. "Uh-huh. Great...."

"But this year I came out of the dugout and knocked one out of the park. The student president is a senior, and he wanted my older brother, Jon, to pinch-hit for me, since Jon's a junior and I'm just a sophomore. But Jon's already run for vice president three times and lost. Three strikes and you're out, right? So I sent him to the showers. Now I'm the vice president, and Jon's just the secretary."

[Riley: Am I losing my mind? Or does this guy talk like a sportscaster?]

He paused and chewed his pizza. "My brother and I don't really get along."

Riley stared at him. She had no idea what he was talking about.

"You know, you're cute, ump," Andrew said, wiping his hands on a napkin. "Do you mind if I call you ump?"

[Riley: Okay, I'm not losing my mind. This guy is a total baseball freak. Or just make that a freak, period.]

"Ump?" Riley asked. "Why do you want to call me that?"

"Short for *umpire*," Andrew explained. "I don't know, it just fits you. Your face kind of reminds me of a baseball diamond. You know, like your nose is the pitcher's mound, your left eye is first base, second is here in the middle of your forehead—" He pointed to the different parts of Riley's face as he talked. "Your right eye is third, and your mouth is home plate!"

Riley's mouth dropped open. She didn't know what to say.

"You've got a little tomato sauce on home plate there, ump," Andrew said. He took his napkin and wiped a spot off the corner of her mouth.

[Riley: You can see why I'm speechless, can't you? This guy can't say a word without direct permission from major league baseball! I guess I can answer my own question now. He's not funny ha-ha. He's funny weird.]

"So how do you think the date's going so far, huh?" Andrew asked. "Hmm? What am I batting here – eight hundred or nine hundred?"

"Is batting nine hundred good?" Riley asked.

"Very good," Andrew replied. "Nobody ever bats nine hundred. It means getting a hit nine out of ten times at bat. Most players are lucky to hit three hundred."

"Oh," Riley said. "Well, in that case, you're not batting nine hundred. More like minus one hundred."

Andrew laughed. He seemed to think Riley was joking. "What are you saying? You're sending me down to the minor leagues?"

"I would never say that," Riley replied. Because I don't talk that way! she thought.

chapter three

"So, today's Tuesday," Chloe said. She sat with Lennon at the Newsstand that evening, sipping a mocha latte. They'd gotten together to study French. It wasn't so easy to get studying done at the popular café, though.

"Tuesday," Lennon repeated. "Yup."

She was hoping to find out what Lennon was planning for Valentine's Day that Friday. Or at least get a hint. But so far he was playing dumb.

"Tuesday's not bad, but it's not the best day of the week," Chloe said. "Which day of the week do you like best, Lennon? I kind of like F*riday*."

"Friday's good," Lennon said. "Saturday's better, though."

"I like Saturday, too," Chloe said. "But sometimes Friday is, you know, special." Come on, come on, she thought. Don't you see where I'm trying to lead you?

Lennon was very smart, but he wasn't so great at picking up on hints.

[Chloe: Last Christmas I wanted this stretchy orange-gold top I saw at the mall. It was shiny and gorgeous, like a goldfish. I dragged Lennon past it every chance I got, hoping he'd get the hint. "Look at that top," I'd say. "Isn't it beautiful?" "Sure," he'd say. "Looks just like a goldfish." By Christmas Eve I was sure he'd figured it out. But what did he end up giving me for Christmas? A goldfish! Close enough, I guess. I named it Clueless.]

Lennon nodded. "This Friday's pretty big," he said.

Yes! Chloe silently cheered.

"This Friday?" she asked innocently. "Oh, really? Why is that?"

Lennon opened his mouth as if he was about to say something. Then he snapped it shut. "No reason," he said, smiling and looking away.

How cute is that? Chloe thought. Lennon won't let me spoil the surprise. What a sweetie! I'm so lucky to have such a thoughtful boyfriend. And I've only got three days to wait until Valentine's Day.

[Chloe: Okay. Three of the longest days of my life!]

Chloe knew exactly how she wanted to spend those three days. If Lennon was planning something wonderful for her, she'd plan something wonderful for him, too. He deserved it.

Her mocha latte was finished. She leaned across the table to take a sip of Lennon's lemon slushie – but she gulped it too fast.

The icy-cold drink shot a piercing pain right to her brain! Her head went all numb. She couldn't think, she couldn't move – she couldn't do anything until the pain went away.

"So, do you think you're ready for the French test on Thursday?" Lennon asked.

"Unnnnghh," Chloe murmured, pressing a hand to her forehead.

"Brain freeze?" Lennon asked.

She nodded.

"I'll wait," Lennon said.

Her brain slowly warmed up, and at last Chloe was able to think again. She liked the way Lennon was used to her little quirks. And that he never told her to stop drinking slushies. She loved the stuff.

"All better?" he asked.

"Better than better." Chloe smiled.

"You ready to go soon?" Lennon asked. "I've got some things to do at home...."

Chloe glanced at the clock on the wall. It was only nine, and she didn't have to be home until ten. "What's the rush?" she asked.

"No rush." Lennon stood up and helped her to her

feet. "It's a beautiful night. Let's take a walk in the moonlight together."

Chloe's cheeks flushed. He kept hold of her hand as they left the Newsstand and headed toward her house. It really was a beautiful night.

"We hardly studied any French tonight," she said.

"That's right," Lennon said. "I was supposed to help you with that, wasn't I?"

Lennon had traveled a lot with his family. He spoke French fluently, as well as Japanese and Italian. He was really good at languages.

"Let's practice a little now," he suggested. "I'll say a sentence and you translate it. Ready?"

"Ready," Chloe said.

"*Je suis une fille très jolie*," Lennon said in his perfect accent.

That was easy. "'I am a very pretty girl,'" Chloe translated.

"*Très bien*. Let's see.... *Il n'y a pas un garçon plus intelligent que Lennon*."

Chloe rolled her eyes. "'There is no boy more intelligent than Lennon.' These are too easy for me, Lennon."

They had almost reached her house. Lennon stopped and said, "How about this one? *Je veux l'embrasser*." He turned to Chloe and gazed into her eyes.

"Um, 'I want to kiss you'?" she asked, not quite sure.

"Very good," Lennon said. "You get a gold star." He leaned down and kissed her softly on the lips.

Chloe's legs felt like butter in the sun. She had to grab his arm to keep from melting to the ground.

"I think I've got my French homework down now," she whispered when he pulled away.

He laughed and kissed her again. Then he walked her to her front steps. "Good night, Chloe," he said.

"See you at school tomorrow," she replied, waving to him as he walked away.

Wow, Chloe thought as she ran up the steps to her front door. Her face was still hot. I think I'm in love!

She watched Lennon until she couldn't see him anymore. Then she opened the door and went inside the house, humming. She found Riley waiting for her in the kitchen, licking the frosting off a pink cupcake. Pepper was asleep on a mat on the floor.

"Pink for Valentine's Day!" Chloe cried, grabbing a cupcake. "I can't wait! How was your date, Riley? Did he ask you out for Friday night?"

Riley didn't look up from her cupcake. "Yes. Yes, he did," she reported.

Chloe clapped her hands. "He did? That's great! What did he say?"

"He said, 'Want to step up to the plate with me this Friday?'" Riley replied.

Chloe stared at her sister. "Step up to the plate? Oh, I get it. That's cute. So what did you say?"

"I said, 'No, Andrew, I don't want to step up to the plate this Friday. I'm yanking you from the lineup.'"

Chloe blinked. "What does that mean? You turned him down? Why?"

"Chloe, did you hear what I just said? The way he asked me out? He talks like that all the time. He uses baseball sayings for *everything*! He called me *ump*! It was unbearable."

"But at least you'd have a date for Valentine's Day," Chloe protested. "It couldn't have been *that* bad."

"It was the worst date ever!" Riley insisted. "After all that, he tried to get to first base with me!"

"Really?" Chloe asked.

"Yes," Riley said. "And after tonight anything with the word *base* in it does not appeal to me. I'd rather stay home and match up all the spare socks in the dryer than go out with a jerk like that – especially on Valentine's Day."

"Riley, you don't mean that," Chloe said.

"Yes, I do!" Riley insisted. "I've had it. No more dating. I'm swearing off boys for at least three months. I declare a *boy*-cott!"

"A boycott – of boys? For three whole months? You'll never last that long," Chloe said.

"Watch me." Riley popped the last bite of her cupcake into her mouth.

Chloe poured herself a glass of milk. She wished Riley had somebody to feel all romantic about, the way she felt about Lennon.

But Chloe couldn't feel bad for long. She started humming again and touched the cool glass to her cheek.

Riley stared at her. "What are you so happy about?" she asked. "Did something happen at the Newsstand?"

"No, nothing really," Chloe said, feeling herself blush. "I mean, nothing unusual."

"But something's up," Riley insisted. "Your cheeks are all red."

Chloe drained her glass of milk and sat down at the table. "It's Lennon," she burst out. "I think I love him!"

"Really? For real?" Riley asked.

Chloe nodded. She couldn't hold it in any longer. "He keeps getting sweeter and sweeter! Tonight he was saying these romantic things to me in French, and he held my hand, and when we kissed goodnight, it was like – pow!"

"Wow," Riley said. "That's awesome! Just in time for Valentine's Day!"

"I know," Chloe said. "It's going to be the most special Valentine's Day ever. And you know what? I think I'm going to do something very brave. Brave, but in the Valentine's Day spirit." She paused and swallowed. She hadn't thought this through yet. It was just coming to her now, like a brilliant inspiration.

"I'm going to tell Lennon how I feel about him on Valentine's Day," she said. "I'm going to tell him I love him!"

Riley's eyes widened. "You're *what*?"

"I'm going to tell him I love him!" Chloe practically shouted. She was so excited, she could hardly wait to do it. She wanted to call Lennon on the phone and tell him right then. But, no, it would be better to wait for the right moment.

Manuelo poked his head into the kitchen. "Hello, my little chickens. What's going on in here?" he asked. "I thought I heard shouting."

Chloe shot Riley a warning glance. Don't tell. Not yet, anyway, she thought. This was too personal. For now, the only person she could confide in was Riley. If Manuelo knew, he'd make a big deal about it – fussing about exactly how Chloe was going to tell Lennon, what she was going to wear, what words she was going to say. He might even tell her mom about it! Pretty soon Chloe would wish she hadn't said a word.

"It's nothing, Manuelo," Riley said. "Chloe was just getting out of hand over your cupcakes."

"They are delicious, aren't they? I think I'll have another one." He crossed to the table and snatched up a cupcake. "I'll be in my room if you need me."

"Okay, Manuelo," Chloe said. "Thanks."

When he was gone, Riley whispered, "I can't believe you're going to tell Lennon you love him! Are you sure you want to do that?"

"Positive," Chloe whispered back. "The more I think about it, the more I want to do it. He's planning something big for me on Friday. I overheard him talking about it, and he mentioned it again tonight.

Some kind of huge Valentine's Day surprise! So I want to surprise him, too. It's perfect timing!"

"Chloe, I'm not so sure that's a good idea," Riley warned.

"Why not?" Chloe asked. "I'm sure he loves me, too. Or pretty sure, at least. He acts like he loves me. And why would he go to so much trouble to surprise me on Valentine's Day if he *didn't* love me?"

"It's just..." Riley paused. "Well, what if you scare him away?"

"You're being negative because you've had a few bad dates lately," Chloe said. "That doesn't mean I should hold back. Not every boy is a jerk. And Lennon's not like other boys."

"Lennon's great," Riley admitted. "I just hope you know what you're doing. Because if you're wrong..." She didn't finish the sentence. She didn't have to.

Chloe shuddered and put the thought out of her mind. I'm not wrong, she told herself. I just know it.

chapter four

"Psst! Riley!" Sierra whispered during earth science class the next day. Riley glanced at Sierra, who was sitting two seats away to her left. Between them sat Larry Slotnick, Riley's goofy next-door neighbor. Larry had once been crazy about Riley. He used to follow her around like a puppy. Sometimes Riley thought he still liked her a little bit.

Then Larry and Sierra had started dating. But they broke up, and now Larry, Sierra, and Riley were all friends.

Sierra reached across Larry's desk and handed Riley a note folded up into a tiny square. Riley's name was written on the front.

"Who's it from?" Riley whispered.

Sierra shrugged. Riley quietly unfolded the note while Ms. Mitchell, the science teacher, droned on.

It was the first day of Riley's "boy-cott," and already she felt good about her decision. Life would be so much easier without boys. Simpler. She felt strong. She read the note. It said:

Dear Riley,
I wish we were lab partners. You shake my molecules.

Riley glanced around the room. Who could the note be from?

Everyone else was looking at the blackboard, where Ms. Mitchell was writing out the names of different types of minerals. Everyone except Barton Blau, who was staring at Riley, his braces glinting in the fluorescent light.

Well, this was something new. Barton Blau was always so busy doing science experiments and math problems he never even seemed to notice girls. Now he was suddenly writing notes to her? What was up with that?

Maybe it's a joke, Riley thought. She was glad she'd declared her boycott. It was a good excuse to say no to Barton. He was nice and everything, but…well, she already had a Larry in her life.

A few seconds later Sierra handed her another note.

Dear Riley,
By the way, that last note was from me, Barton. Except I'm going by Bart now.

Yours in atomic passion,
Bart

Riley sighed and stole another glance at Barton. Was it a joke? He crooked and uncrooked his index finger in a little wave at her. Riley had a feeling Barton wasn't kidding. She looked away and pretended to concentrate on Ms. Mitchell. But before long another note arrived.

Dear Riley,
I love your eyes. They're so blue. Did you know blue eyes are a recessive gene? By the way, will you go out with me on Friday night?
Your admirer from afar,
Barty
P.S. Please write back.

Riley folded up the note. This was terrible! What was she going to say?

Someone tapped her left arm. It was Larry. He gave her another note.

Dear Riley,
What's going on? What's with all the notes?
—Larry

Riley showed him Barton's latest note. She watched him while he read it. Barton and Larry were sort of similar. Barton had braces, and Larry had a retainer. Barton had greasy brown hair, and Larry had spiky brown hair. Larry's eyes were close together, and Barton's were wide apart, but they both had the same hopeful expression.

Larry shook his head and wrote her another note.

Dear Riley,
I can't believe what some guys will do to go out with you! Barton's really lost it. By the way, you look especially gorgeous today. That blue dress really brings out your eyes. No wonder Barton noticed them. I meant that in a neighborly way, of course.

Your friend,
Larry

P.S. You'd better send a note back to the poor guy or he'll never stop writing you. Not that I know from experience or anything.

—L

Riley grinned. Larry was goofy, but he was never dull.

She tore a small piece of paper out of her notebook and wrote:

Dear Barton,
I wish I could go out with you. I really do. Unfortunately, I just made a vow not to date any boys at all. I can't break this vow. If I do, I'll lose all respect for myself. You wouldn't want that to happen, would you? I mean, could

you live with yourself?

Riley

She folded up the paper, wrote Barton's name on it, and passed it toward him. She watched out of the corner of her eye as he read it. Her heart sank as he busily wrote her another note.

Dear Riley,

Your vow only makes me love you more. I will respect it, though. Please tell me when, if ever, you change your mind. I will be waiting and watching you with love-filled brown eyes. Brown eyes are a dominant gene.

Bart

When the bell rang, Riley grabbed Sierra's hand and hurried her out of the room before Barton could catch up to them. Larry tried to tag along.

"Sorry, Larry – girls only," Sierra said.

"But I already know what's going on!" Larry protested.

"It's okay, Sierra," Riley said.

"So what's with all the notes?" Sierra asked.

Riley showed her Barton's notes.

"Your boycott couldn't have come at a better time," Sierra said.

"Tell me about it," Riley agreed. "The weird thing is, ever since I declared my boycott last night, boys seem to be throwing themselves at my feet. It's only lunchtime, and Barton is the third one today!"

"You're kidding!" Sierra cried.

"Gee, I wonder why," Larry said sarcastically. "That is *so weird*...."

"Okay, Larry, now you have to go," Riley said.

"I need a snack anyway," Larry said, starting down the hall. "My blood sugar is dropping fast."

"Who else threw himself at you?" Sierra asked when Larry was gone.

"Some kid I don't even know started flirting with me on the school bus this morning. And that guy who works at the fruit stand on the corner – what's his name?"

"Craig?" Sierra said.

Riley nodded. "I stopped to buy an orange, and he carved a heart in it with a knife." She traced a heart shape in the air with her index finger.

Sierra raised her eyebrows. "Weird."

Chloe and Tara came running up to them as they headed for study hall.

"Riley! You won't believe what I just heard!" Tara cried.

"What?" Riley asked.

"Well, these two girls were talking – seniors," Tara explained. "And one of them said she'd been teasing Hunter McKenna about the girl he liked."

"Hunter McKenna?" Riley repeated. He was a senior and the hottest guy in school by a mile. Tall, athletic, wavy black hair, and a killer smile. "Who does he like?"

"Well, he wouldn't tell her at first," Tara said. "But she finally got him to admit it was a *ninth grader*."

Riley stopped to take this in. The idea that Hunter could be interested in a ninth grader was surprising – and extremely juicy.

"So?" Sierra prompted. "Who is it?"

"It's Riley!" Tara cried.

"Do you believe it?" Chloe said.

"What? No way!" Riley said. Hunter McKenna liked *her*? Her heart started pounding. She couldn't help it. This was exciting.

"*Yes* way," Chloe insisted. "Tara heard it in the bathroom!"

[Riley: Everybody knows that the girls' bathroom is the best source of news and gossip in any school. And most of the stuff you hear there is really true. At least Tara says it is. I guess for some reason you can't make stuff up when you're surrounded by ceramic tile and chrome.]

"Oh, please," Riley said, playing it cool. She tried to calm herself down, but her heart kept on pounding. "It's just a rumor. Hunter doesn't even know me. We've never said a word to each other."

Still, if it *is* true... she thought. Hunter McKenna! That would be wild!

The bell rang. "I've got to meet Amanda in the cafeteria," Chloe said.

"We'll go with you," Riley offered. She could be

late for study hall. Ms. Suarez never noticed.

They went into the cafeteria and found Amanda waiting for Chloe at their usual table.

"Did you hear the big news?" Chloe asked Amanda, and she quickly filled her in.

"That's amazing!" Amanda said.

"Oh, but too bad about your boycott," Chloe added.

"My what?" Riley said.

"Your boycott," Chloe repeated. "The one you just declared last night?"

"Oh, yeah," Riley said. It had come in handy all morning, but suddenly it didn't seem so convenient anymore. Hunter McKenna! Every girl in school would kill to go out with him! What if he really liked her?

"I'm sure the rumor isn't true," Riley said.

"But what if it *is* true?" Sierra pressed. "What would you do? You wouldn't pass up a chance to go out with Hunter just because of some silly boycott – would you?"

"Let's wait and see if he actually asks me out," Riley said. "Then I'll tell you."

Sierra rolled her eyes. "Give me a break. You'd go out with him in a second."

Inside, Riley really *wasn't* sure what she'd do. And she didn't want to seem too eager. Besides, Chloe would never let her hear the end of it if she dropped her boy-cott so quickly, after the big speech she'd made the night before and everything.

"Change of subject," Riley said. "Chloe, did you find out anything else about Lennon's big surprise yet?"

Chloe shook her head. "Not yet. But I know something's up. I asked him if he wanted to go out to dinner with me Friday night, and he said sure. He said to go ahead and make a reservation somewhere, just not too early...because he has *something important* to do that afternoon!"

"Aha!" Riley said. "The surprise."

"I wonder what it is," Tara said.

"Maybe he's organizing a singing telegram," Sierra said.

"I wish I knew," Chloe said. "I can't stand the suspense!"

Riley didn't blame her – she was getting curious about Lennon's surprise, too. "Well, I guess I should get to study hall," Riley said, and she started for the exit.

Suddenly Tara stopped and nudged her.

"Hey – look who it is," Tara said.

Riley turned toward the side door. There stood Hunter, scanning the cafeteria as if he was looking for somebody.

"Get ready," Chloe said. "Something tells me it's time to put your boycott to the test."

Wow, Riley thought. Is he looking for me? Is he really going to ask me out?

chapter five

Riley swallowed. "He could be looking for anybody," she said. But she had to admit, part of her hoped Hunter was looking for her. He was so gorgeous! The way he stood leaning in the doorway with his arms crossed, staring out from under the hair hanging into his eyes...

"We'd better get to study hall," Sierra said.

"Yeah, Riley," Tara said. "Time for study hall. Come on, let's go out *that* way." She pointed to the door where Hunter stood.

"I'll come, too," Chloe said.

"Me, too," Amanda added.

They all headed for the cafeteria exit.

Hunter stopped Riley. "Hey – isn't your name, like, Riley?" he asked.

Riley gulped and nodded. So it was true!

"Can I, like, talk to you a minute?" he asked.

"Sure," Riley said.

Chloe, Amanda, Tara, and Sierra circled them, waiting to hear what Hunter would say. He pulled Riley away and said, "Alone?"

Chloe, Tara, Amanda, and Sierra giggled and left the lunchroom. Riley could see them peeking through the window in the door.

Riley pulled herself together. Here we go, she thought. "What's up?" she asked.

Hunter grinned at her. His teeth gleamed, perfect and white. Maybe this is it, she thought. Maybe this is the perfect guy for me – my Lennon. No more jerks and no more dry spell!

"Would you, like, like to, like, go out with me on, like, Friday night?" Hunter asked.

"Friday night?" Riley asked. "You mean, this Friday?"

"Uh-huh." Hunter nodded.

Wow! Riley thought. He's asking me out for Valentine's Day! Hunter McKenna! I feel like Cinderella!

She felt as if the top of her head might fly off, she was so excited. But the thought of her boycott stayed in the back of her mind, nagging at her.

Am I really that spineless? she wondered.

Now that she was actually faced with breaking her vow, she felt a little bad. She didn't want to let herself down.

Riley stared into Hunter's brown eyes. She was torn. He was so gorgeous. But she'd sworn off boys! What about her self-respect?

"You're, like, real cute." He smiled again, gazing back into her eyes and flashing his perfect teeth.

She could hardly speak. She was lost in his eyes and in her own thoughts. Come on, Riley, she told herself. Just say it. Just say you can't go. Maybe you can ask him if he's free in three months – when your boycott on boys is over. Just do it!

"Maybe, like, you're, like, busy," Hunter went on.

Riley felt a twinge, an irritation, like the bite of a mosquito. She snapped out of her trance. Something was annoying her. It annoyed her so much, it pulled her out of her dreamy staring contest with Hunter.

"Wait a second," she said. "Say that again?"

"I said, like, maybe, like, you, like, already have, like, a date," Hunter said.

The hair prickled on the back of Riley's neck. What was he doing? Why was he talking that way?

[Riley: I don't mind when people say "like" once in a while. I do it myself. But this guy uses it every other word! I wouldn't be able to stand talking to him for more than five minutes—I don't care how cute he is!]

Well, at least this makes it easier to say no to such a hottie, Riley thought. After all, she *was* boycotting boys!

"I'm really sorry, Hunter," Riley said. "But I already did make plans for Friday night. It was nice of you to ask me, though."

She didn't bother telling him what she would be busy doing – hanging out with Manuelo, eating red and pink foods all night. That was, like, none of his business.

"Cool," Hunter said, but his smile faded.

Riley had the feeling Hunter didn't hear "no" very often.

"See you around," he said, and he left.

Chloe, Tara, Amanda, and Sierra rushed back into the cafeteria.

"What happened? What did he say?" Tara asked.

"He asked me out for Friday night," Riley told them.

"Wow! Valentine's Day! He must really like you!" Sierra said.

"I guess," Riley replied. "But I'm not going."

"What?" all four girls said at once.

"I'm on a boycott, remember?" Riley said. "And that means *all* boys. Even cute ones."

Chloe shook her head. "You're nuts. I still say the boycott won't last."

"I don't know," Sierra said. "Turning down Hunter was pretty impressive."

"Wait and see," Riley said. "This is just the beginning."

"Hi, Chloe," Manuelo said, walking into the kitchen later that day. He opened the refrigerator and pulled out some chicken. "Learning anything interesting from the back of that cereal box?"

"Yeah," Chloe said. She was sitting at the kitchen table having an after-school snack of cereal and milk. "Fruity-O's have one hundred percent of the daily allowance of niacin my growing body needs." She continued to stare at the back of the cereal box, but she wasn't really paying attention to it. Her mind was on Lennon – and what she wanted to tell him on Valentine's Day.

"Interesting," Manuelo said. He coated the chicken with a marinade and put it back into the fridge. Then he picked up the Fruity-O's box and studied it. "I see it's also full of riboflavin."

Chloe stared at Manuelo. She decided to ask his advice.

"Manuelo? What would you do if you were going to say something really special to somebody? I mean, how would you do it?"

"What are you talking about?" Manuelo asked. "I need more details than that to answer your question."

Chloe took a deep breath. "Okay, but if I tell you, you have to promise not to say anything to anybody – except Riley," she told him. "It's really personal."

Manuelo scooted into the seat next to her and smiled. "I promise. Tell me," he said.

"Well..." Chloe began. She took another deep breath. "I love my boyfriend," she announced, "and I'm going to tell him on Valentine's Day."

Manuelo raised his dark eyebrows. "That *is* a big deal," he said. "If you're going to do something that big, you've got to do it right."

"I know!" Chloe said. "That's why I'm asking your advice."

"Well, for a situation like this, the most important thing is to set the mood," Manuelo said. "You can't tell someone you love him outside a gas-station rest room – you know what I'm saying? You need a romantic atmosphere."

"Yeah, you're right," Chloe said. "Atmosphere."

"In the right atmosphere you can pull off just about anything," Manuelo said. "Candlelight, maybe a nice restaurant."

"Exactly," Chloe said.

She could picture the scene in her mind: she and Lennon sitting across from each other in a romantic candlelit restaurant, eating delicious food. She says, "I love you, Lennon," and he says, "Oh, Chloe, I've been waiting to hear you say those words! I love you, too, more than I can say…."

Well, maybe it wouldn't happen quite like that, but something along those lines.

Manuelo pulled the phone book off the top of the fridge and set it on the table in front of Chloe. "Why don't you try La Boulette de Viande? It's the best restaurant in town, and very romantic."

"Thanks, Manuelo." Chloe opened the phone book and ran her finger through the restaurant listings in the yellow pages. "La Boulette de Viande – aha! Here it is."

"Rats!" Manuelo cried. "I forgot to get jalapeño peppers at the store. Without them my famous Chicken Manuelo tastes like paper! Do you need anything, Chloe?"

"No, thanks," Chloe said.

"Good luck with the restaurant." Manuelo took his car keys from a hook by the kitchen door. "See you later." He hurried out to the car.

Chloe dialed the restaurant's phone number.

"*Bonjour*, La Boulette de Viande." A man with a French accent answered the phone. "May I help you?"

"Hello," Chloe said. "I'd like to make a dinner reservation for two, please."

"What day?" the man asked.

"This Friday," Chloe replied.

The man on the phone began to laugh. He laughed and laughed and laughed. Finally he said, "You want a reservation for Valentine's Day? We were booked up two months ago!" He laughed again.

That made Chloe angry. "Good for you!" she snapped. "You know what? I'm glad you're booked up. Your restaurant is too stuffy anyway!" She hung up, his laughter still ringing in her ears.

What a jerk! she thought. So I'm a little late with my Valentine's Day plans. He didn't have to get such a kick out of it. But his reaction worried her – maybe it wouldn't be so easy to get a dinner reservation for

Valentine's Day. Why had she waited until the last minute?

Because I didn't realize I was in love until the last minute, she thought. Her heart started racing. Was she really going to do it? Was she really going to tell a boy for the first time ever that she loved him?

Yes, she told herself firmly. Yes, I am really going to do it.

But it had to be perfect. Everything had to be just right. Even Manuelo had agreed.

La Boulette de Viande wasn't the only restaurant in town. Her favorite restaurant was a little Italian place called Maria's. She dialed the number.

"I'm sorry, miss. We're all booked up that night," the reservation person said.

Okay, so that didn't work, Chloe thought. I'm not going to get discouraged. There's got to be someplace in town we can go for Valentine's Day. Maybe it doesn't have to be perfect, just good enough.

She dialed another restaurant, and another, and another. But it seemed as though every restaurant in town was already booked. She even tried California Dream, the café on the beach where she and her friends liked to hang out. It was supercasual, but at least it was something. But even that didn't work – they were having a private party that night!

"Oh, no!" she groaned, dropping her head into her hands. What was she going to do? Take Lennon to Chuck E. Cheese?

"Hey, Riley. Wait up!"

Riley turned around to find Nick Tracy, grinning and jogging toward her. She was just on her way out after a tough day at school. "Hi, Nick," Riley said. "What's up?"

"Oh, nothing," Nick said. He stood in the hallway, staring at his feet.

Riley waited for him to say something else. To explain why he had stopped her for no apparent reason.

[Riley: Now, let me just tell you that Nick has never stopped me to talk before, ever. He lives down the street from us. When we were little, he used to ride his bike around and around the block, but I don't think he ever noticed me – or Chloe – before, except to make mean comments on the fact that we were girls. You know, something clever like, "Eeww, yuck, girls stink!" But now that he's not a little kid anymore, he's kind of cute.]

"So, are you going home now?" Nick asked. "I could walk with you. Because, you know, I live right in your neighborhood."

[Riley: Is it me, or do you get the feeling that he's going to ask me out, too? Why, oh, why can't this happen when I'm NOT staging a boycott on boys?]

"Yeah, I know," Riley said. "Well, thanks, Nick, but I'm not going home yet. I've got something to do...this after-school activity thing...." Riley racked her brain, trying to come up with an excuse not to walk home with Nick. The way he was looking at her, he'd probably ask her out before they even got outside. And a couple of days ago she might have said yes. But now she was determined to stick to her boycott – even though Nick was looking cuter by the minute.

"How about doing something this weekend?" Nick pressed. "Want to go surfing or something?"

"You surf?" Riley asked. "I love surfing!" It might be fun to go surfing with Nick, she thought. But he'd probably think of it as a date. No. I have to be strong! "I'd better not – I've got tons of homework to do this weekend. But thanks – it was nice of you to ask."

"Oh. Okay," Nick said. "Well, maybe next week."

Riley nodded. "Sure. Maybe." She didn't feel like getting into the whole boycott thing with Nick. He'd never understand.

Way to go, she said to herself, mentally patting herself on the back. Way to stick with the boycott. She was proud of herself for turning down a cute guy like Nick. But it was getting harder and harder to say no. For one thing, coming up with excuses wasn't so easy. What she needed was a distraction, something to fill up her free time and give her a good reason not to go out on dates.

As she started down the hall, she spotted Barton making a beeline for her. Oh, no, she thought. Not again…

"Hi, Riley," Barton said when he caught up with her. "Did you know there's a four o'clock showing of *Bugs from Space* at the mall today? If you're not busy – "

"Sorry, Barton," she said, glancing desperately around the hall for some kind of excuse. Then her eye fell on a poster on the activities bulletin board.

DJS WANTED FOR KWMH, THE WEST MALIBU HIGH SCHOOL RADIO STATION. AUDITIONS WEDNESDAY AFTERNOON FROM 3:00 TO 4:30 AT THE STUDIO. SEE SKIP DAVIS, STATION MANAGER.

The radio station was brand new. Riley had read about it in the school paper. It was going to be student-run and broadcast in the mornings before school, during the school day, and after school until five. DJs could use study halls, free periods, and even some class time to broadcast their shows.

Aha, Riley thought, glancing at the clock. It was Wednesday and it was 3:30. Perfect.

"Riley?" Barton asked. "*Bugs from Space*?"

"I'd love to, Barton, but remember what I told you about my vow? Anyway, I can't today," she said. "I've got to audition for the radio station – *right now*. See you!"

She hurried down to the new radio studio in the school basement. She stopped in front of the door to see if Barton had followed her. He hadn't. All clear.

Then she opened the station door and saw a long line of...boys.

A short, chubby senior with pale hair and a clipboard smiled at her. "Hi, I'm Skip," he said. "Are you here to audition?"

The boys all turned to look at her. Why not? Riley thought. She'd be a DJ! It would be fun!

She nodded.

"Good," Skip said. "We need girls. For some reason radio attracts mostly guys."

Uh-oh, Riley thought. I hope this wasn't a mistake.

Skip handed her another clipboard and a pencil. "While you're waiting to audition, write a paragraph describing what kind of show you'd like to do. It can be music, interviews, call-in – whatever you want."

Riley sat down and waited her turn. What kind of show would she like to do? She didn't have to think about it for long. Definitely music, she decided, listing some of the songs she'd like to play.

Finally Skip called her into the soundproof studio. "Read this short news announcement," he said, handing her a piece of paper.

Riley sat down, put on a chunky pair of headphones, and spoke into the microphone.

"'Good morning, West Malibu!'" she read. "'In school news, today's field trip to Paramount Studios is canceled due to lack of permission slips! Get with the program, people!'"

She felt shy at first, but as she read she grew bolder. "'Ms. Morton's English classes will be having a substitute teacher today. Get those paper airplanes ready.... It's Wednesday, and you know what that means – meatloaf for lunch. The rest of today's menu: green beans, rice, veggie burgers...'"

This is fun, she thought. She liked the feel of the headphones on her ears and the sound of her voice coming through them. And the new studio was very cool, with all the latest equipment.

I'm glad I stumbled into this, she thought. I really hope I get a spot!

"That was great, Riley," Skip said when she was finished. "You read well and have a nice voice. Why don't you sit in the waiting room for a few minutes? I've got two more auditions to hear, and then I'll assign some of the time slots. We want to get started right away."

"Thanks," Riley said. She took off the headphones and went into the waiting room. All the chairs were already taken, so she sat on the floor and listened to two boys talking behind her.

"Dude, I'm calling my show *Get Mr. Connor*," one boy said. Mr. Connor was the vice principal. "He's given me detention one too many times. My show will be one hour of nothing but insults about the guy!"

"Cool," the other boy said. "You could take calls from other dudes who got detention, too."

"Yeah," the first boy agreed. "We're going to totally ruin his day."

I hope they don't give that guy a show, Riley thought. She wasn't Mr. Connor's biggest fan, but a whole show as revenge for detention? It didn't seem like a very good use of radio time.

"Okay, everybody." Skip came out of the studio with his clipboard. "The auditions are over, and here's what I've got. Jason Willensky, I'm giving you the after-school music slot from three to five."

"All right!" Jason slapped the hand of the guy sitting next to him.

Skip read out some more assignments. The boy who hated Mr. Connor didn't get one. Riley started to get nervous. What if she didn't get a slot either?

Finally Skip said, "Riley, I'd like to give you the morning show."

Riley jumped up. "That's excellent!" she cried.

"It's a big responsibility," Skip added. "I think it will be our most popular slot. I figure kids will listen to it on their way to school."

"Thank you, Skip," Riley said. "I won't let you down." She paused, staring through the studio window at all the equipment – levers, knobs, buttons, and meters. "There's only one problem," she said. "I have no idea how to work all that stuff."

"No problem," Skip said. "I'm going to pair you with someone who knows the soundboard." He knocked on a door marked OFFICE. The door opened and out stepped a lanky guy with long brown hair, black jeans hanging loose off his hips, heavy dark-framed glasses, and a black T-shirt that said THE BLOODENING in dripping red letters.

"What's up?" the guy asked.

"Charlie, this is your new partner, Riley Carlson," Skip said. "Riley, this is Charlie Slater. He's our most experienced DJ. You guys are going to be the morning team."

> **[Riley: I know, I know. I started this whole radio thing to avoid boys, not be partners with one. But now I really want to be a DJ! It looks like fun. And there's something kind of cool about Charlie. Don't worry, I'll stick to my boycott. It might get a little tough, but I can do it.]**

Riley braced herself. If Charlie was like most of the other guys she'd run into that day, he'd be drooling all over her within ten seconds. But she was ready. She'd tell him their relationship had to stay purely professional, since they were working together and all....

Charlie raised one hand in a limp wave. "Hey, Riley. What's the word? Skip, can I talk to you for a minute?"

Charlie pulled Skip aside and whispered, loud enough for Riley to hear, "I don't need a partner, man. I had my own show on a local station last year!"

"I think you two will be good together," Skip said. "And Riley needs someone to help her learn the technical stuff. Come on, just try it out."

"She looks too...mainstream," Charlie said.

This was too much for Riley. "Mainstream?" she protested. "What's wrong with that? So what if I like popular music? So do most of the kids in this school. And anyway, how can you tell if I'm mainstream or not? You don't even know me."

Charlie squinted at her through his glasses. "I can tell just by looking at you. Straight blond hair. Clothes right out of the mall. No tattoos or piercings. Total cheer-leader type."

Riley scanned him for tattoos and spotted one peeking out from the short sleeve of his T-shirt. It was a mermaid. Not very original, she thought.

"For your information, I'm not a cheerleader," She said. "Not right now, anyway. And even if I were, what's wrong with that?"

"Like I said," Charlie repeated. "Mainstream."

Well, at least her boycott was safe. There was no chance she'd ever want to go out with *this* guy. She didn't want to be partners with him, either.

"You're a snob," Riley shot back. "I can tell *that* just by looking at *you*. And you're just the kind of snotty jerk I can't stand! Sorry, Skip. Looks like this won't work out after all."

She tried to storm out the waiting-room door, but it was hard because she had to step over the legs of all the guys sitting on the floor.

"Riley, wait a second!" Skip called. "Listen to me."

Riley stopped at the door.

"Why don't you two just give this a chance?" Skip pleaded. "I need both of you. You'll make a great team. Riley, you need Charlie because he's a good engineer. He knows how to work the equipment, and he also knows music."

"I know she needs me, but I don't need her," Charlie said.

"That's not true," Skip said. "You'll need her to make your show lighter, more fun, more popular with the kids. I'm telling you, the two of you together will have the best show on the station. And unless one of you quits, you're stuck together."

"Hey, man, I'm not quitting," Charlie said. "This station needs me. I'll be the only DJ with any soul, any integrity. Without me KWMH will feature just a bunch of teenyboppers."

"Well, I'm not quitting, either," Riley said, changing her mind. No way would she let Charlie push her out of her DJ slot. She'd auditioned and won the spot fair and square. He didn't scare her. She'd show him *mainstream*.

"Good," Skip said. "It's settled. Start planning your show and be ready to go on the air Friday morning."

chapter six

"Ohhhhh, no. No. I am *not* playing that," Charlie said. He picked up Riley's Beyoncé CD and tossed it on the floor. "Riley, the kids depend on us. We've got to play good stuff for them, not the junk they hear on big corporate radio stations. Next."

Riley stared at the pile of rejected CDs on the floor. It was Thursday afternoon, and she and Charlie were in the studio, planning their first radio show. It was not going well. So far Charlie had said no to every song Riley suggested.

"I think the kids will want to hear music they like," Riley protested. "Not just songs *you* like."

"They don't *know* what they like," Charlie said. "Bunch of robot clones." He showed her a tiny MP3 disk. "Here's some great stuff I recorded off the Internet. You can't even buy this stuff yet. This will knock their socks off."

He slipped the disk into a player. Loud noises blasted out of the speakers. Riley couldn't tell what was making the noises. Not a guitar, that was for sure. Then a male voice started screeching. Riley put her hands over her ears.

"Turn it off!" she shouted. She pressed the off button herself. "We're *not* playing that."

"Yes, we are," Charlie insisted. "Look, I know what I'm doing here. I'm in tenth grade, and I've DJ'd before. You haven't even been a DJ for one day yet. So watch the master and learn."

Riley's mouth fell open. She couldn't believe how arrogant Charlie was! She glanced at the list of ideas she'd jotted down in her notebook the night before. "Well, if you won't play any of my CDs, at least let me name the show," she said.

Charlie sighed. "Let me hear what you've got."

"*Rise and Shine with Riley and Charlie*," Riley said.

Charlie rolled his eyes. "First of all, it should be *Rise and Shine with Charlie and Riley*," he said. "But no, I'm not doing a show with a silly name like that."

"What would you like to name it, Mr. Genius?" Riley snapped.

"Something like *Morning Death Rant*," Charlie said.

"No." Riley had to put her foot down somewhere, and this looked like the place. "Absolutely not. I'm not naming my show *Morning Death Rant*."

"Well, I'm not naming my show *Rise and Shine with Regis and Kelly*, or whatever it was you suggested," Charlie shot back. "End of story."

Riley crossed her arms and stared at the table covered with CDs, fuming. The more she knew Charlie, the less she liked him. No, it was more than that. She couldn't stand him!

How would they ever work together on the air? And how would they get a show together by tomorrow morning? she wondered.

"Ugh, sloppy joes," Chloe groaned as she stood in line at the cafeteria on Thursday afternoon. She'd forgotten to bring her lunch that day, so she had to eat school food. She preferred to eat "cute" food – small, neat, bite-sized foods that weren't messy. That way, if a boy saw you eating, you could look cute and not piggy. But sloppy joes were about as far from cute food as you could get.

"Pssst! Chloe!"

Chloe felt someone tap her on the arm. She turned around. "Lennon, you don't have lunch now!" But she was glad he was here.

"I know," Lennon said. "I got out of art early. I already finished my project." He took her hand. "Come with me," he said, leading her out of the lunch line. "I know you don't want to eat this slop. I've got something better for you."

Hmmm – art project, Chloe thought as she followed him to a table in the back corner. Could that be connected with the surprise somehow? Valentine's Day was the next day, so the timing was right.

"Ta-da!" Lennon said. He had set up a special lunch, complete with plastic plates and forks.

Chloe peered into a plastic container. "Your mother's lasagna!" she cried. Lennon's mother made fantastic lasagna.

"That's right," Lennon said. "We had a lot left over from dinner last night, so I brought an extra serving just for you, garlic bread and all. I even cut it into cute little bite-size pieces for you."

"Lennon, that's so sweet!" Chloe exclaimed. "What a nice *surprise*!" She gave him a meaningful look on the word *surprise*, but he didn't seem to get it.

"Glad you like it," he said.

They sat down to eat. "This is delicious," Chloe said. "Speaking of surprises," she began. "About tomorrow night – "

"Friday!" Lennon said. "The weekend at last."

"Uh, yeah," Chloe said, confused. T*he weekend*? Didn't he even remember it was Valentine's Day? Or was he just teasing her?

"Anyway, I thought we could meet on the beach," Chloe said. "At seven. For a moonlight picnic. What do you think?"

It was the best Chloe could come up with. All the restaurants were booked. But once she got used to the idea of a picnic, she thought it might be nice. More romantic than a restaurant any day.

"Sounds good," Lennon said. "I'll be there."

With a surprise? Chloe wondered. He smiled at her, and her heart swelled. She loved him! She wished she could say it right then and there. But no, it was better to wait.

Just wait until tomorrow, Lennon Porter, she thought. Have I got a surprise for *you*!

"The picnic sounds perfect, Chloe," Quinn said. "Most boys don't like restaurants anyway."

"That's true," Tara said. "They get all stiff in those fancy chairs and the different glasses and silverware and everything. They can't relax."

Chloe was roaming the mall with Tara and Quinn after school on Thursday.

"I hope so," Chloe said. "Anyway, I have no choice. It's either a picnic or Mickey D's."

She wanted to say more, but she hesitated. She was so excited and nervous about telling Lennon that she loved him, and she was dying to tell Quinn and Tara about her secret plan. But she stopped herself. If she told everybody about it, it wouldn't be secret anymore. And Tara did kind of have a big mouth. It would be awful if Lennon heard about it before she had a chance to say the words. That would spoil everything!

"Have you gotten any more clues about his surprise?" Quinn asked Chloe. "What do you think it is?"

"I have no idea," Chloe said. "Lennon doesn't know that I know he's planning something, so I can't just come out and ask him. I have to tiptoe around the subject. But I guess I'll find out once and for all tomorrow."

"What about you?" Quinn asked. "Are you getting him anything?"

"I was thinking about it," Chloe said. "After all, he's working up some kind of big surprise for me. I want to have a little gift for him, too."

"What kinds of things does he like?" Tara asked.

Chloe sighed. "I have no idea. Boys are impossible to shop for."

"There must be something in the mall he'd like," Quinn said.

They passed shop after shop. "What about something like that?" Quinn asked, pointing to a short-sleeved bowling shirt in a window.

"He already has a million of those," Chloe said.

She stopped in front of another store. A T-shirt in the window caught her eye. It was white with words in black letters all across the front. The first words, in English, were KICKIN' IT. Then the phrase was translated into every language Chloe could think of – French, Latin, German, Chinese, Russian, Indonesian, Finnish....

"That's it!" Chloe cried. "That's the perfect shirt for Lennon. He loves foreign languages, and it looks totally cool."

"So go buy it," Tara said, pushing Chloe into the shop.

Chloe approached a young sales guy. "I'd like to see that T-shirt in the window," she said. "Do you have any fresh ones?"

"That's our last one," the sales guy said.

Chloe glanced at Quinn and Tara. "I'll take that one then," she said. "I hope it's a medium. I think that's his size. Right, Tara?"

"Probably," Tara said. "Or maybe a large."

The sales guy got the shirt and checked the tag inside the collar. "This one's a small," he said.

Chloe studied the tee more closely. It was definitely too small for Lennon.

"Are you sure you don't have any more?" she asked.

"Positive," the guy said. "Sorry."

Rats, Chloe thought, disappointed. The shirt was perfect!

"Will you be getting any more in by tomorrow?" Chloe asked hopefully.

"I don't think so," the guy said.

"That's too bad, Chloe," Quinn said. "It really would have been perfect for Lennon. But this one will never fit him."

"Do you know where I might find another one like it?" Chloe asked the sales guy.

"They're imported from England," he said. "We're the only store in town that carries them."

"Now what am I going to do?" Chloe asked her friends. "Nothing is going to be as good as this shirt. But I have to get him something."

"Maybe he'd like one of those instead," Tara suggested. She pointed to a pile of T-shirts with different slogans and designs on them.

Chloe riffled through the pile. The shirt from the window would have been a special present because it was so perfect for Lennon. These other shirts were… just shirts.

"He's planning a big surprise for me, and all I'm getting him is a dumb T-shirt," she said.

"What can you do?" Quinn said. "You've got to get him something, and you don't have time to shop around. Valentine's Day is tomorrow."

"I know," Chloe said.

"Just get him one of these," Tara said, patting the pile of T-shirts. "He'll like it, I promise."

Chloe found one with a cool psychedelic pattern on it that she thought Lennon might like. "I guess I'll get this," she said, choosing a medium.

"It's a cool one," Quinn said.

"At least you found something," Tara said.

Chloe glanced at her watch. It was almost six. "I've got to get going," she said. "Manuelo is picking me up in a few minutes. I'm supposed to go to Lennon's house to study tonight."

"Sure," Quinn said. "*Study.*"

"We really do study," Chloe insisted.

"See you at school tomorrow!" Tara said.

Chloe hurried downstairs, through the atrium, past the fountain, and out of the mall. Manuelo was waiting by the entrance in the car. She hopped into the front seat.

"Look what I bought for Lennon for Valentine's Day," Chloe said, showing Manuelo the T-shirt.

"Nice," Manuelo said. He pulled away from the curb and drove home.

"What's for dinner tonight, Manuelo?" Chloe asked.

"My famous baby pizzas and a salad," he said. "I thought you'd like a quick dinner since you're going out later."

"Thanks, Manuelo," Chloe said. "That sounds perfect."

A few minutes later they pulled into the Carlsons' driveway. The phone was ringing when they walked into the house.

"I'll get it!" Chloe called. She ran to the phone and picked it up.

"Hey, Chlo, it's me," Lennon said. "Sorry, but I've got to cancel our study date tonight."

"Why?" Chloe asked.

"Uh – something came up," Lennon said. "I'm sorry, I can't really talk about it right now. But you'll find out about it soon."

"Soon?" Chloe repeated. "How soon?"

"Well, tomorrow, I guess," Lennon said.

Tomorrow! Chloe tingled with excitement. He must be working on her surprise! "That's okay," she said, trying not to sound too excited. "I'll study with Riley tonight."

"Thanks for being so cool about it," Lennon said.

"No problem," she said. "See you tomorrow... valentine."

"See you tomorrow," Lennon said.

Chloe hung up and went to her room. Riley wasn't home yet, so she had the room to herself for a while.

I hope this surprise is good – really good, she thought – after all this buildup. But of course it would be. She knew it would be.

Chloe sighed. Valentine's Day was looming large in her mind. Things were good with Lennon, and she loved him. She was pretty sure he loved her, too. But more and more it seemed as if everything was riding on one moment – the moment when she said those three little words to him.

She imagined the two of them on a picnic blanket under the stars. The moon glowed on the ocean and on her wavy blond hair. Lennon brushed a stray strand from her face. "I love you, Lennon," she said. He leaned toward her and kissed her. The music swelled....

Well, maybe there wouldn't be swelling music, but everything else would be perfect. The food, the moonlight, the ocean, the stars, even the blanket. This was going to be one of the biggest moments in her whole life!

She clicked on her radio and started wrapping Lennon's present.

"And now for the weather," the radio announcer said. "Tonight, clear and warm, a low of sixty-five degrees. Tomorrow, increasing clouds with a chance of rain by midnight. A high of seventy-five. Chance of rain, ninety percent."

Rain? Tomorrow night? It hardly ever rained in Malibu! Chloe groaned and collapsed on her bed.

It can't rain tomorrow night. It just can't! she thought. *If it does, my Valentine's Day picnic will be ruined. My romantic atmosphere will be gone. How can I say the L-word to Lennon without that?*

chapter seven

"Good morning, dudesters," Charlie said into the microphone after the *Morning Death Rant* theme music ended. "Or should I say, *bad* morning."

"Actually, I think *good* morning works fine," Riley said into her mike.

She and Charlie sat in the booth at the radio station on Friday morning, broadcasting their very first show. Riley loved it already. If only Charlie wasn't around to ruin everything!

"No, *bad* morning," Charlie insisted. "This is the best show at West Malibu High, *Morning Death Rant* – "

"Also known as *Rise and Shine with* – " Riley cut in.

"No, it's *not*," Charlie said. "This is *Morning Death Rant*. And I'm Charlie, spinning the tunes with my co-host, Riley. Bad morning, Riley."

"Bad morning to you, too," Riley snapped. And she meant it.

"We'll be playing some music that will make your curly hair straight and your straight hair curly. This next song is called 'Drive-Thru Funeral Home.'"

Charlie put a CD into the player and reached for the play button.

"No, it's not," Riley said. "We're not playing that stupid song."

"It's not stupid, Riley," Charlie said. "It's – "

"Charlie's just joking," Riley said to the radio audience. "Our real next song is called 'The Rain Makes Flowers.'"

Charlie snorted. "Not in my lifetime."

Riley tried to take Charlie's CD out of the player and put hers in.

"Stop that!" Charlie said. He slapped her hand away.

"Ow!" Riley cried.

Charlie pushed the play button, and "Drive-Thru Funeral Home" blasted over the airwaves.

"You're ruining the show!" Charlie said when they were off the air. "Just go along with what I say."

"I won't!" Riley insisted. "*You're* ruining the show!"

It went on like that for the rest of the hour until the show finally ended. Their show was broadcast during the hour just before school started. Riley and Charlie had permission to be late for homeroom to give them time to finish up the show and pack up their gear.

What a disaster, Riley thought. Skip was waiting for them outside the sound booth. He probably can't wait to fire us, she thought.

Charlie and Riley left the booth.

Skip broke into a huge grin. "That was excellent!" he cried. "Kids kept stopping by during your show to tell me how much they love it!"

"Really?" Riley said. "But all we did was fight!"

"Exactly! It was hilarious!" Skip said. "Keep it up. *Morning Death Rant* is a big hit!"

"Excellent," Charlie said. "I told you I know what I'm doing."

"It's not called *Morning Death Rant*," Riley said. "It's called *Rise and* – oh, never mind."

I give up, Riley thought. I can't believe our show is a hit! I love it – but why does it have to be with Charlie?

"Riley! Your radio show was so funny!" Chloe said when she saw Riley and Sierra during a break later that day. They sat under a tree in the courtyard. "Everybody's talking about it."

"Thanks," Riley said. "It's not what I wanted to do, but Charlie is so stubborn!"

"I think he's kind of cute. By the way, how's your boycott going?" Chloe couldn't resist teasing Riley a little bit. She'd made such a fuss about her boycott, and now she'd be spending every morning with a cute guy!

"My boycott is just fine, thank you." Riley sniffed. "And it's in no danger of being broken – trust me."

"Well, you guys are great together!" Sierra said. "And I kind of like the music Charlie plays. I haven't heard most of it before."

"Hey, everybody! Happy Valentine's Day!" Quinn bounded over to them. "Look – I got a valentine from a secret admirer!"

She showed them a homemade card made out of red construction paper. Someone had glued a picture of a duck on it and written *I'm Quackers over Quinn*!

"Ooh," Sierra said. "Who do you think it's from?"

"I have a funny feeling it might be a joke," Quinn said. "From Tara. But I'm not sure."

"Have you seen Lennon yet today?" Riley asked Chloe. "Did he give you a card or anything?"

"Nothing," Chloe said. She tried not to show how disappointed she was. "Not even a kiss. We walked to school together this morning, listening to Riley's radio show. But he didn't say a word about Valentine's Day!"

She knew they were supposed to celebrate together later, at dinner, but still.... She was so nervous about what she wanted to say to him. A little kiss or a card would have given her a boost of confidence.

"That's weird," Sierra said. "Maybe he's holding back until later. For the surprise."

"I hope he didn't forget," Riley said.

"Forget!" Chloe cried. "I hope he doesn't forget to meet me on the beach tonight – if it doesn't rain."

She glanced up at the sky. Ominous black clouds were rolling in. No, no, no, she prayed. Please don't rain! Please don't rain!

* * *

"Stupid weather report," Chloe said to herself that evening on the beach. "It was wrong – thank goodness."

She spread out a big blanket on the sand as the sun was setting over the ocean. It was warm and clear. A shower had drifted through town in the late afternoon, but by five o'clock the sun had burned away the clouds, leaving a sparkling evening.

This Valentine's Day dinner is going to be perfect, Chloe said to herself. She opened her picnic basket and started setting things up. She had a lantern with a candle in it for light, so they could see what they were eating. She got out two plates, napkins, silverware, and a bottle of sparkling apple juice to drink from Champagne flutes. For dinner she'd brought Manuelo's famous barbecued chicken, which tasted even better cold. She'd cut it into small "cute" pieces so it wouldn't be too messy. She also brought potato salad, carrot sticks, and chocolate-dipped strawberries for dessert. Everything was ready. Now all she needed was Lennon.

She watched the sun disappear over the horizon. She checked her watch. It was seven-thirty. Lennon was supposed to meet her at seven. He was late!

Where could he be? Chloe wondered. She turned around to see if he was walking toward her from the road. No sign of him.

I know I told him where to meet me, she thought, getting more frustrated by the minute. What was he doing? Why did he have to pick tonight of all nights to be late?

She lit the lantern and waited some more. And waited. And waited. By eight o'clock the moon was rising, and Chloe was getting worried.

Could he have forgotten after all? she wondered. He hadn't said a word to her about Valentine's Day all day. Had he somehow forgetten what day it was?

Finally Lennon ran down the beach toward her. He plopped onto the blanket, out of breath.

"Are you all right?" she asked. "We were supposed to meet at seven!"

"I know. Sorry I'm late!" He kissed her and added, "I would have called you to explain, but I couldn't. It was a secret."

Chloe sat up straight. The surprise! She couldn't wait to find out what it was.

"What secret?" she asked him. Finally, she thought. Finally I'll find out what my surprise is!

chapter eight

"Get ready," Lennon said. He had a big grin on his face. "I, Lennon Porter...won the state science fair competition!"

"That's nice," Chloe said. "But what's the surprise?"

Lennon's grin faded. "*That's* the surprise," he said. "I made the best science fair exhibit in the whole state of California. It's a big deal. Aren't you proud of me?"

"Oh – *oh*!" Chloe said. It finally dawned on her what he was saying. She was too confused to know how she felt, exactly. But she knew she should at least act a little excited.

"Of course I'm proud of you," Chloe said. "It's just – that's not what I was expecting you to say."

What *was* I expecting him to say? she wondered. And what should I do now?

He took her hand. "I'm sorry, Chloe. Happy Valentine's Day." He gave her a kiss on the cheek. "I'm sorry I was late. The state finals were held in San Diego this afternoon. I just got back."

That's why he was late. San Diego was a two-hour drive away. Chloe tried to keep her disappointment from showing, but it wasn't easy. Instead of brain freeze she was getting heart freeze. She couldn't help it. The surprise had nothing to do with Valentine's Day – or her – at all. Did Lennon love her? Did he even care about her? Maybe telling him she loved him tonight wasn't such a great idea after all....

"I rushed to get here as fast as I could," Lennon went on. "But you know, it's Friday, and there was a lot of traffic. Plus the award ceremony and everything."

Chloe tried to perk up. Her boyfriend had just won the state science fair, and she was sulking! Of course he was excited, she thought. And I should be, too.

"What was your project?" she asked. "Was that the big secret you've been keeping all week?"

Lennon nodded. "I invented a better 'mousetrap.' I used a chemical extract of cat smell and turned it into a spray! The smell keeps mice away without hurting them. It's perfect for animal-rights activists who don't want mice in their homes."

"That is a great idea," Chloe said.

"Anyway, enough about that. It's Valentine's Day, and I have something for you," Lennon said. He handed her a small box wrapped in silver paper and tied with a red ribbon. "I hope you like it."

A present! Here was the thoughtful Lennon she knew.

"Thanks!" Chloe said. She opened the box. Inside was a very pretty coral and silver bracelet.

Wow! A Valentine's Day gift – and of jewelry, too! That was a good sign.

"It took me weeks to pick it out," Lennon said. "I even brought my mom to the mall with me one time."

He was so sweet! Chloe thought. Her romantic feelings started welling up inside her again.

"Lennon, it's beautiful!" She threw her arms around his neck and kissed him.

"Glad you like it," he said.

She slipped it onto her wrist. It was very elegant and felt cool on her skin.

"It looks great on you," Lennon said.

"I have something for you, too," Chloe said. She'd almost forgotten. She gave him his present, wrapped in red and white paper. Lennon grinned and opened it. "Cool T-shirt," he said. "Thanks, Chloe. It will go great with jeans and stuff."

"You're welcome." She wished she could have given him something better, like the other T-shirt, but what could she do?

"Look at everything you brought!" Lennon exclaimed. He finally noticed the beautiful moonlight picnic Chloe had set up. "What have you got to eat? I'm starving."

She opened the picnic basket and served him some chicken, carrot sticks, and potato salad. She poured them each a glass of sparkling apple juice.

"To you," Lennon toasted. "The cutest valentine in Malibu."

Chloe clinked glasses with him, her heart melting fast. They leaned against each other, eating the chicken, gazing at the moon and the stars, and letting the warm breeze from the ocean waft over them.

Once she'd gotten over her disappointment about his surprise, Chloe realized she was having a perfect Valentine's Day after all. She touched the bracelet on her wrist.

"Hey – did you see that?" Lennon pointed at the sky. "A shooting star!"

Chloe followed his finger and caught the last second of a flash across the sky. She made a wish.

I *will* tell Lennon tonight, she thought. I have to. This is the perfect time.

But first dessert.

She cleared away the dinner things and pulled out the chocolate-covered strawberries.

"Lennon..." she began.

"Yes?" He sat up and looked into her eyes.

Chloe hesitated. Just do it, she told herself. Can't you see the way he's looking at you? Go for it!

He picked up a strawberry and popped it into his mouth.

"Lennon...I want to tell you something," she said.

He nodded. "What's up?"

"Um...Lennon – " She swallowed. This was it. "Lennon, I...I love you."

Chloe stared at his face in the lantern light, trying to read his expression. Her heart pounded. What would he say?

He looked down at the picnic blanket and picked at a thread.

Chloe's heart beat faster. What was wrong with him? Why wasn't he saying anything?

Another minute went by. Had he heard her?

Come on, say something! Chloe thought.

Finally he reached down and picked up another strawberry. He popped it into his mouth.

"Did you make these yourself?" he asked, his mouth full. "They're really good."

chapter nine

Chloe's mouth went dry. That was it? That's all he had to say?

She'd poured out her heart to him, told him she loved him, and he munched on strawberries as if nothing had happened!

She waited one more second to make sure that was all he had to say – to give him a chance to save this whole sorry mess at the last minute.

He didn't take it.

Chloe felt tears welling up in her eyes. Whatever she did, she was *not* going to let him see her cry. She had already humiliated herself enough.

She got to her feet.

"Chloe? What are you doing?" Lennon asked.

She didn't answer. Choking on tears, she ran up the beach, stumbling in the sand.

"Chloe, what's wrong?" Lennon shouted. "Come back!"

She didn't look back. She just ran as hard as she could.

She could hear him puffing through the sand behind her. I won't let him catch me, she thought, speeding up. He won't see me cry. And I never want to see him or talk to him again!

She ran all the way up the steps from the beach to her house. When she got to the top, she stopped to look back.

Lennon was far behind, chasing her up the beach. He waved his arms at her. "Chloe! Stop! Let me talk to you."

Not on your life, she thought. She ran onto the back deck, out of his sight. Through the sliding glass door she saw Riley, Manuelo, and Pepper in the kitchen, celebrating Valentine's Day together.

Riley and Manuelo were frosting heart-shaped sugar cookies with red icing and eating raspberry sorbet. Pepper watched with her tongue hanging out. They looked so safe and happy. So not embarrassed.

Not like me, she thought. I just totally humiliated myself in front of my boyfriend!

Chloe slid open the door and stepped inside.

"Chloe!" Riley cried. "What are you doing back so soon?"

Manuelo stepped closer. "Uh-oh," he said, staring at her face. "You've been crying."

"Crying!" Riley dropped her frosting knife into the bowl and ran to Chloe's side. "What's the matter?"

"Where's Lennon?" Manuelo asked.

"Out on the beach," Chloe said. "If he comes to the door, don't answer it! I mean it!"

"What happened?" Riley asked.

"I told him I loved him," Chloe admitted.

"And?" Riley asked.

"What did he say?" Manuelo asked.

"Basically he said, 'I really like these chocolate-covered strawberries!'" Chloe wailed.

"Oh, no. Come sit down, Chloe." Manuelo put an arm around her shoulders and led her to a chair at the kitchen table.

"Why? Why, oh, why did I have to tell him I loved him?" she cried. "I'm so stupid!"

"Don't be silly," Manuelo said. "It's a mistake anyone could make."

"He doesn't love me," Chloe said. "That's obvious. If he did, he would have said, 'I love you, too.' And everything would be great now. We'd be out on the beach drinking sparkling apple juice and wishing on shooting stars."

"Chloe, don't beat yourself up," Riley said.

"I can't ever look him in the face again," Chloe said. "I've totally humiliated myself."

The doorbell rang. Everyone froze.

"I'll answer it," Manuelo said at last.

"Manuelo, no!" Chloe jumped up and barred the way out of the kitchen. "Let's pretend we're not home!"

"But he's sure to see the lights on," Riley protested.

"I don't care!" Chloe insisted. "Let him think whatever he wants. I can't see him! I can't!"

The doorbell rang again. Riley sneaked upstairs and peeked out the bathroom window to make sure it was Lennon. It was. He was banging on the door with his fists now, calling, "Chloe, let me in!"

"Come on, Chloe, talk to him," Manuelo said. "You have nothing to be ashamed of. All you did was express your feelings. You're a passionate person – you should be proud! He is the one who should be embarrassed. Obviously he has all the soul of a wilted piece of lettuce...."

"No, no, no!" Chloe said. "I can't do it. It's too awful."

After a while the ringing and knocking stopped.

"Is he gone?" Chloe asked.

Riley checked. "He's gone. But he's going to come back. And you can't avoid him at school. You'll have to face him sometime, Chloe."

Chloe buried her head in her hands. "I know, I know," she moaned. "What am I going to do?"

The next night Chloe and Riley went to the Newsstand to see Sierra's band, The Wave, perform. But Chloe couldn't help looking at the door every few minutes.

"Oh, no – is that Lennon?" Chloe asked when the door opened. She ducked behind Riley and peeked over her shoulder toward the café entrance.

"Relax – it's somebody else," Riley said.

"Maybe we shouldn't have come," Chloe said. Lennon worked at the Newsstand, but he had the night off. Still, he might show up to see The Wave play – and Chloe didn't want to see him. She was still upset about what had happened the night before. She'd thought he loved her! But obviously he didn't.

"He'll probably show up later to celebrate his science award," she added. "And then what will I do?"

"Just be cool," Riley advised.

The Wave took the stage. "Hey, everybody!" Sierra called out. "Thanks for coming!" They started their first song.

Chloe glanced at the door again. Still no sign of Lennon. Whew! Maybe he wouldn't come after all.

Tara, Amanda, and Quinn squeezed in at Chloe and Riley's table. "Cool shirt!" Quinn called to Chloe over the music.

"Thanks," Chloe said. She was wearing a pale yellow blouse she'd just gotten at the mall.

Heads bobbing, they watched the band. By the third song all the girls were on their feet dancing. After the last song the whole café was on its feet in an uproar, cheering and yelling for more.

"You guys were great!" Chloe said when Sierra joined them at their table. "Better than I've ever seen you."

"You really rocked," Tara agreed.

"It's too bad more kids don't know about you,"

Chloe said. "You could play bigger clubs than this, easily."

"Thanks," Sierra said. "But there are lots of great bands around. It's hard to spread the word, you know?"

"Hey, wait a minute," Riley said. "I know how to spread the word – by radio! I've got a radio show now, and we need to fill airtime. We could use *Morning Death Rant* to promote local bands – starting with The Wave!"

"Really?" Sierra jumped to her feet. "That would be so cool!"

"I could play a cut from your demo CD on the show next week," Riley said. "Soon everyone at school will know your songs, and they'll spread the word even farther!"

"Thanks, Riley!" Sierra said. "That's so excellent! I'm going to go tell everybody."

She ran over to the table where Alex, Marta, and Saul – the other members of The Wave – were sitting. Riley and Alex used to go out, but now they were just friends. Chloe wondered if she could ever be just friends with Lennon. That night it felt impossible.

"That really is a great idea, Riley," Chloe said. "Although I'm not sure The Wave's music qualifies as a *Death Rant*."

Riley rolled her eyes. "Charlie can't have his way about everything. He's always trying to boss me. But it's my show, too. Anyway, I bet he'll love The Wave once he hears them."

The café door opened again. Chloe couldn't help looking up to see who came in. This time it *was* Lennon.

"Hide me!" she pleaded, sliding down in her seat.

Riley tugged her back up. "Come on, Chloe," she said. "You've got to face him sometime."

Chloe kept her eyes glued to Lennon as he went to the coffee counter. He hadn't spotted her yet. He ordered, and soon the counter girl gave him an iced coffee. He put milk and sugar into it. Then he turned around – and saw her.

Their eyes locked for a second. Chloe quickly looked away.

"Chloe!" Lennon called. He rushed across the room toward her.

"Oh, no!" Chloe said. "Here he comes!"

He stumbled over a chair. Chloe watched it all happen as if it were in slow motion. The iced coffee flew out of Lennon's hand. He fell across the table. And the iced coffee splattered all over Chloe's new yellow shirt.

The whole café saw it – and the place erupted in laughter.

I don't believe this! Chloe thought, tears stinging her eyes. He's humiliated me again!

She knew he hadn't done it on purpose, but it didn't matter. All her fantasies about Valentine's Day and what would happen when she told Lennon she loved him had been crushed. He didn't love her. So what was he hanging around for?

"I've got to go," Chloe said. She got up and ran out of the café, the crowd's laughter ringing in her ears.

chapter ten

"Chloe, wait!" Lennon called after her. "I'm sorry!"

I don't care, Chloe thought. She just wanted to get out of there – and away from him.

"Chloe, stop!" Lennon called again.

But Chloe didn't stop. She ran all the way home.

[Chloe: Maybe you think I'm crazy, running away from Lennon like this. The thing is, have you ever had a whole café laugh at you? It's no picnic. Well, maybe it is like one kind of picnic – the kind where your boyfriend practically comes right out and says he doesn't love you.]

Riley walked into their bedroom a few minutes later. "Chloe, are you okay?"

"Yes," Chloe said. She'd changed into an old T-shirt and thrown her stained shirt into the wastebasket.

"Chloe, I'm sure Manuelo can get this stain out,"

Riley said, lifting the pale yellow shirt out of the basket.

"I don't care," Chloe said. "I don't want it anymore."

"Lennon didn't mean to spill his coffee on you," Riley said. "He just wanted to talk to you."

"It doesn't matter," Chloe said. "He humiliated me two nights in a row! Right now I've got to stay away from him."

"But you love him," Riley said.

"I know," Chloe said. "That only makes it worse!"

"That was 'Supersize It' by the Shakes," Charlie said into the microphone. "You liked that one, didn't you, Riley. I saw your head bopping."

"It rocked," Riley said into her mike. "And the lead singer's really hot."

"You're so lame," Charlie teased. "You like any band if the lead singer's hot."

"That's not true," Riley protested.

"It's 8:32 on Monday morning," Charlie said. "This is KWMH, and you're listening to *Morning Death Rant* with Charlie and Riley. This next song is a Riley pick – well, I just turned her on to it this morning, but she said she wanted to play it. Tell it to the people, girl."

"'You Scratched My Bike' by the Orange Crates," Riley announced.

She pressed play, and the music blared. She and Charlie grooved along to the song while they got the next set ready.

Riley was really getting into this DJ thing. Charlie wasn't so bad once you got used to him. She kind of liked fighting with him. And she even liked some of the songs he played. She was learning a lot about how the equipment worked and hearing all kinds of new music.

"That's our show for today," Riley said when their time was up. "See you tomorrow – same bat time, same bat channel."

"Till then – keep up the rant!" Charlie said.

"I'm not crazy about our sign-off," Riley said into the mike.

"We're working on it, kids, we're working on it," Charlie added. "Over and out."

He put on the next DJ's theme music and they left the studio.

"That wasn't bad," Charlie said as they picked up their books in the lounge outside the studio. "Not bad at all. You're coming along, Riley."

"Well, we've still got some kinks to work out," Riley said. "I had a great idea over the weekend."

"Oh, no," Charlie said. "Okay, I'm bracing myself. What is it?"

"Why don't we have a short segment once a week where we play local bands?" Riley suggested. "We'd be doing a service to the community and giving the bands around here some publicity. We could start with The Wave."

"The Wave?" Charlie sneered. "No way. I can't stand them. They're too pop. All the other local bands are lame, too. Believe me, I go to shows. I've seen them all."

"Come on, Charlie, it's a great idea," Riley insisted. "The kids at school will get really excited if they hear their friends on the air."

"Forget it," Charlie said. "I'm not playing lame music for any reason. Just because some kids who go to West Malibu High are in a band is not a good reason to ruin our show by playing them. I will *never* play The Wave on my show." He pushed open the studio door and headed for class. Fuming, Riley watched him walk down the hall.

Just when I was starting to like him, she thought, he gets all obnoxious again!

What's that? Chloe wondered as she approached her locker that afternoon. Somebody had stuck something onto her locker door. From down the hall she couldn't tell what it was. It just looked like a yellow splotch.

When she got closer, she realized it was a rose with a note taped to it.

The front of the note said C*hloe* in Lennon's handwriting.

Maybe he's changed his mind, Chloe thought, getting excited. Maybe he realized that he loves me, and he wants to tell me in a love letter!

Chloe's hands shook as she opened the note. Please be a love note, she prayed. That was the only thing that would make her feel better. Anything less just wouldn't cut it.

If he doesn't say he loves me now, Chloe thought, then he clearly doesn't. And I just can't be with a boy who doesn't love me but knows that I love him! It's too embarrassing.

She read the note.

> Dear Chloe,
> Why are you so mad at me? I don't understand. Please accept this rose as a token of how I feel about you.
>
> Lennon

He didn't sign it *Love, Lennon*, Chloe thought. So what is he talking about? How does he feel about me?

She plucked the rose off her locker and sniffed it. It smelled nice, but it was kind of wilted. Half-dead, really. If this rose was supposed to symbolize how he felt about her, it wasn't a good start.

Then she remembered what Manuelo had told her about roses and their meanings. Yellow meant friendship – *not* love! Was that what Lennon was trying to say? Was he trying to rub it in that she loved him and he didn't love her?

How could he do this to her? When had Lennon gotten so mean?

chapter eleven

"That was the Troggs," Charlie said into his mike Tuesday morning. "An oldie-but-goodie garage-rock single from the sixties."

"And here's a newie but goodie," Riley said, popping The Wave's CD into the player. She kept the cover hidden from Charlie so he wouldn't know what it was. "I know you'll all like it. All of you."

Charlie gave her a funny look, but he didn't say anything.

She just knew he'd like The Wave if he gave them a chance. But she also knew that if *he* knew this song was by The Wave, he'd say he hated it without even listening to it.

He's so closed-minded, she thought. He's always trying to "open my ears" and get me to like new stuff. Well, I'm going to open *his* ears for once.

Charlie got up and rummaged through his bag of CDs, looking for something. The Wave's first song started to play. Riley nodded along to the music, smiling. Charlie didn't look over at her. At last he sat down again with some CD cases in his hand. The song ended.

"Well, kids, I don't know what *that* was," Charlie said into his mike, "but I sure didn't like it. And I don't usually play that kind of poppy stuff on my show, as my loyal fans know. I apologize for Riley's bad taste."

B*ad taste*! Riley glared at him. Who was he to say she had bad taste! She was so mad, she couldn't speak.

[Riley: What is it with guys and music? Why do they always have to declare that the music they like is the only good music and that everything else is garbage? Why can't they just live and let live?]

"Uh, Riley? We've got dead air here," Charlie said. "You want to tell us who played that nerd-song you just spun?"

Riley pulled herself together. "That was a great local band called The Wave," she announced. "They're actually pretty popular."

"Yeah? Well, not with me. You want to hear a good song? I'll play you a good song. I just need a minute to find it. In the meantime, here's something new from Jack Johnson."

He put on some music and dug through his pile of CDs, still looking for something.

Riley stared at him for a few seconds, furious. "How could you do that?" she finally demanded. "You just insulted my friends over the air!"

"How could *you* do it?" Charlie snapped back. "I told you I didn't want to play them on my show, and you did it anyway! My fans will think I'm losing my touch!"

"This isn't just *your* show, you know," Riley said. "It's my show, too!"

"You don't know what you're doing," Charlie said. "You're still learning. Aha!" He held up a CD by a band called Mean. "Here it is. Now *this* is good music."

He took the CD out of its case. Suddenly Lennon burst into the radio station and waved at them through the big glass studio window. He pointed to Charlie.

"What?" Charlie said, even though Lennon couldn't hear him. "I'm busy here."

"It's important," Lennon said, moving his mouth slowly so Charlie could read his lips.

"I'll be right back," Charlie said to Riley. "Put something on – anything but The Wave."

Riley made a face at him behind his back.

"I saw that," Charlie said.

Riley put on another CD. She watched through the window as Charlie and Lennon talked. Lennon looked kind of upset. Charlie nodded. He came back into the booth and started looking for another CD. Disks were spread out, loose, all over the studio now.

"What did Lennon want?" Riley asked.

"A favor," Charlie said. "You'll see."

He found a CD and dropped it onto the messy pile of disks in front of him. The song Riley had put on ended.

"I don't usually do this," Charlie said into his mike, "but I have a special dedication to make. Chloe, this is for you – from Lennon."

He pushed some buttons on the console and reached for a CD from his pile without really looking at it. There were so many CDs there, Riley could hardly tell which was which.

He popped the disk into the player.

Riley picked up a CD case and stared at the cover. Oh, no, she thought. I hope this isn't the CD he's about to play.

Chloe stood in the hallway, listening to Riley's radio show on her Walkman. "Chloe, this is for you – from Lennon," she heard Charlie say. She straightened up in shock. Lennon was dedicating a song to her! What did this mean?

She braced herself. What if this turned about to be another disappointment, like the yellow rose?

But she couldn't help hoping. What if this was the way he finally managed to say it – with a love song?

She closed her eyes, waiting to see what song Lennon had chosen for her. A loud punk song started playing. Chloe was surprised. Lennon wasn't a big punk fan. The singer slurred his words, so she couldn't understand much of the first verse. But then the chorus blasted into her ear, loud and clear.

"I *hate you, go away*! I *hate you, go away*! *You stink, so why don't you just – go away*!"

Chloe's eyes flew open. All around her kids were hanging out in the halls before school, listening to *Morning Death Rant* – and hearing Lennon humiliate her *again*!

She yanked off her headphones and clicked off the radio. That was it. She'd had enough. She didn't need to have a heart-to-heart with Lennon, like everybody was telling her. And he clearly didn't want to apologize to her.

"Okay, Lennon," she whispered. "I got the message."

It was too loud to ignore.

"What are you doing?" Riley shouted at Charlie as the punk song "I Hate You, Go Away!" played. She was furious with Charlie and with Lennon. How could Lennon request such a mean song? And how could Charlie go along with it? Didn't he realize how much it would hurt Chloe's feelings?

"First you insult my friend Sierra and her band on the air, and now Chloe! I don't care if Lennon asked you to do it – you still shouldn't have done it! Take this CD off right now!"

"I can't just yank a record off in the middle of a song!" Charlie protested.

She stared at him. How could she ever have liked him? He cared more about his stupid radio show than about people's feelings!

She loved the radio show. But she couldn't let Charlie use it to insult her sister and her friends! She had to take a stand. There was only one thing she could do. "I can't work with you anymore," she said. She stood up and walked out. "You're impossible! I quit!"

chapter twelve

"There he is," Tara said. "Go get him, girl."

Chloe stood at the lunchroom entrance. She'd been looking for Lennon all morning, but she hadn't seen him – until now. There he was, sitting at a table with Zach and Sebastian, laughing and eating as if nothing was wrong.

Well, something *is* wrong, Chloe thought. You're about to get a chicken potpie in your face!

She marched up to Lennon's table. He grinned when he saw her. "Hi, Chloe!" he said cheerfully. "Did you listen to *Morning Death Rant* this morning?"

Chloe's jaw dropped open. She couldn't believe his nerve!

"Yes, I did," she muttered.

He grinned even more broadly. "Did you hear my dedication? How did you like it?"

"Here's how I liked it," Chloe said. She picked up his carton of milk and dumped it on his head! Then she mashed his half-eaten chicken potpie into his face.

"What?" Lennon sputtered under a coating of milk and veggies. "What was that for?"

"I never want to see you or speak to you again, Lennon Porter," Chloe said.

"Why?" he asked. "What did I do wrong?"

She turned on her heel and stormed away. What did he do wrong? As if he didn't know!

"Boys are the worst," Chloe said that night after dinner.

Riley sighed. "I never knew how bad they could be until I met Charlie."

"I thought Lennon was different," Chloe grumbled. "What an idiot I was!"

"They're all bad," Riley said. "Except for you, of course, Manuelo."

"Thanks, girls," Manuelo said. "You'll get over this someday, Chloe. In the meantime, have some more cupcakes. I made too many for Valentine's Day, and I didn't have such a big celebration after all."

"Tell me about it," Chloe said, biting into a cupcake.

The phone rang. "Will you get it, Riley?" Chloe asked. "I'm screening."

"Well, I'm screening, too," Riley said, looking at Manuelo.

"All right, I'll get it. But I can tell you who it is without even checking the Caller ID." Manuelo stood up and answered the phone. "Hello? Carlson residence, home of the blues."

Riley and Chloe waited to hear who was calling. Manuelo looked at Chloe and said, "Oh, hello, Lennon. Let me see – "

Chloe frantically shook her head and whispered, "No! No! I'm not here!"

"I'm sorry, Lennon," Manuelo said. "Chloe's out. Sure. I'll tell her you called…again."

Manuelo hung up and returned to the table. "That's the fourth time he's called tonight, Chloe," he said. "Why don't you talk to him? Maybe he wants to apologize."

"I don't think so," Chloe said. "He probably has a new and improved way of humiliating me." She sighed. "Why are guys so afraid of love?"

Riley shrugged.

"Well, Lennon is not going away," Manuelo warned. "And you can't dump milk on his head every time you see him."

"I know," Chloe admitted. But the longer I can put off talking to him, the better, she decided. Riley's boy-cott was beginning to make a lot of sense to her. A *lot* of sense.

"This is *Morning Death Rant*. Bad morning to you all. Wake up, you sleepy West Malibuans! I know it's only 7:45, but I don't care. Let's party!"

Riley sighed as she listened to Charlie's voice on her portable radio. A loud punk song played, and she turned the volume down.

"The show's not the same without you, Riley," Sierra said. They were standing in the hallway with Chloe and Quinn Thursday morning before school. Riley couldn't stop herself from listening to *Death Rant* even though she was mad at Charlie.

"It's no fun anymore," Sierra went on. "Everybody says so. Charlie by himself is just a big bore."

"She's right," Quinn agreed. "The two of you together were so funny! I liked listening to you argue about what songs to play. And the show needs more variety. When Charlie's alone all he plays is punk, punk, punk."

"At least he's not taking dedications anymore," Chloe said.

"What's happening with Lennon?" Quinn asked. "Have you heard from him since the radio disaster?"

"He calls me all the time," Chloe reported. "And he E-mails me. But I won't take the calls, and I delete the E-mails without reading them."

"Why?" Sierra asked. "Don't you want to know what he has to say?"

"I did, once," Chloe said. "But not anymore. What if I open his E-mail and it says something mean? Like, 'Dear Chloe, I live to embarrass you. Making you look like an idiot makes life worthwhile.'"

"I can't believe he'd write something like that," Quinn said.

"But I never thought he'd dedicate a song called 'I Hate You, Go Away!' to you, either," Riley said.

"That's what I'm talking about," Chloe said.

"And now, party people, let's kick things up a notch," Charlie's voice said on the radio.

Riley shifted. She felt restless. She hadn't been doing the radio show for very long, but her mornings felt empty without it.

"I miss *Morning Death Rant*," she admitted. As soon as she said it, she realized it was true. She missed doing the radio show. But why? Charlie was such a jerk! Some of the time, anyway.

"Maybe you can get a show of your own," Sierra suggested. "An afternoon show. By yourself."

"Maybe," Riley said. "But it wouldn't be the same. I miss working with Charlie."

[Riley: Wait a sec. Did I just say that out loud?]

"You do?" Chloe said. "I thought you were mad at him!"

"I am," Riley admitted. "But I still kind of miss him."

"That makes *no* sense," Quinn said.

"I know," Riley said. "I shouldn't miss him. He's arrogant and obnoxious and his hair is too long and all he ever wears are those stupid black jeans and black high-tops and black T-shirts with logos of bands you've never heard of on them. I shouldn't miss him," she repeated with a sigh. "But...I do."

• • •

"Chloe! Wait!"

Chloe didn't have to turn around. She knew that voice. Lennon.

"I've got to talk to you!" he called.

She had just stepped out of the cafeteria after lunch. Lennon was running toward her down the hall.

I've got to get away from him, she thought. Who knows? He could be carrying a stink bomb or something!

She raced down the hall and slipped into the library. The library was pretty big, and she thought she could lose him among the stacks.

She ran to the back and hid in the poetry section. From there she could see the library door. It opened, but the boy who walked in wasn't Lennon.

After a few minutes she figured she was safe. She'd given him the slip.

I'll hang out here a little longer, she thought, just to be safe. She sat down at a desk and stared at the computer screen. The cursor blinked at her. Might as well check my E-mail, she decided.

[Chloe: What? A girl's got to stay connected, no matter what kind of crisis she's in!]

She logged on. Another message from Lennon. Subject: *Please read me*!

She stared at the screen for a minute. Maybe I *should* read it, she thought. It was tempting. What if he had something nice to say for a change? Something that would make her feel better?

No, she scolded herself. Don't fall into that trap again! That's what you thought when he left you the evil yellow rose. When he dedicated a mean song to you. When you told him you loved him.

Telling Lennon I loved him was the biggest mistake of my life, Chloe thought. It was supposed to be a good thing – something to bring us together. How could such a nice thing make everything so awful?

Her hand hovered over the mouse. She clicked on Lennon's message. Then she pressed delete.

chapter thirteen

"Riley, we're going to be late," Chloe called through the bathroom door on Friday morning.

"I know," Riley said. She opened the door and stepped out, a towel wrapped around her hair. "I'll hurry."

Chloe slipped into the bathroom, and Riley went into their bedroom to dry her hair. She flipped on the radio. One of her favorite songs, "Girl in My Soup," was playing.

"That's weird," Riley muttered. "I thought I had the radio tuned to the school station." She checked the number on the radio. It was tuned to KWMH, just as she'd thought. But *Morning Death Rant* should be on by now, she muttered to herself, checking the clock. And Charlie would never play "Girl in My Soup." He hates that song.

The first song ended and a new song came on, "Jumpstart," by Ben Benson, one of Riley's favorite singers.

Okay, now I'm in the twilight zone, Riley thought. Either that or Charlie is out sick today.

But once the song ended, Charlie's voice spoke over the air. "Bad morning to all of you out there in high school land," he said. "No, you're not dreaming. Yes, you are tuned to *Morning Death Rant*. Or maybe I should call it *Rise and Shine with Charlie*."

Now he's going to make some sarcastic comment about the songs he just played, Riley thought, bracing herself. It's got to be a joke.

But Charlie talked on, and Riley didn't hear any sarcasm in his voice. Then he said, "This next band is a local fave – they even go to West Malibu High. And they're playing this Saturday night at the Newsstand. Should be a kick. This is The Wave."

One of The Wave's songs started playing. Riley had to sit down.

Did Charlie just announce The Wave's next show without making fun of it? What was going on?

Chloe burst into the room. "Riley, are you listening to the *Rant*?"

"I thought I was," Riley said. "But it can't be real. Is that really Charlie?"

Chloe sat beside her on the bed. "I was listening in the bathroom. He actually played Ben Benson. I thought he hated pop."

"He does," Riley said. "I keep waiting to hear what the big joke is."

He played two Wave songs in a row, followed by a

folksy pop tune Riley had once wanted to play on the show. He wouldn't let her. So why was he playing it now?

"All right, kids, I've got an announcement to make," Charlie said.

"This is it," Riley said to Chloe. "Here comes the punch line."

"A few days ago a friend of mine asked me to play a song for someone special. A dedication. I didn't want to admit it before, but I made a mistake. I had so many CDs lying around, I accidentally picked up the wrong one and played 'I Hate You, Go Away!' instead of the song my friend asked for."

Chloe gripped Riley's hand. "I don't believe it," she whispered.

"Don't get me wrong," Charlie went on. "'I Hate You' is a killer song. But it's not the message my friend wanted to send. So I'm doing the dedication over again, and this time I'm going to do it right. This song is from Lennon to Chloe. It's called – "

He swallowed, and Riley had the feeling the next words were hard for Charlie to say.

"It's called 'Cutie.'"

A sweet love song played.

Chloe put her hands to her mouth. "I love this song!" she gasped.

"I guess this is what Lennon meant all along," Riley said. "He never hated you or wanted you to go away."

"This explains a lot," Chloe admitted. "But it doesn't explain everything. Not yet, anyway."

It was nice of Charlie to fix his mistake, Riley thought. And admit he was wrong. I didn't think he could do that.

When "Cutie" ended, Charlie said, "Now I have another dedication to make. This one is from me to my former partner, Riley. The show was a lot more fun when she was on it. And I'm not the only one who thinks so. Yeah, I've read your E-mails, kids. A*nd* the threatening notes you taped to my locker. We all want Riley to come back. So, Riley, this is for you."

Music played, a song called "Missing You."

"Wow," Chloe said. "You know what, Riley? I think Charlie likes you!"

And then it hit Riley like a cinder block to the head. It seemed impossible. It *was* impossible. But it was true!

No, please, I don't want it to be true! Riley thought. He's not my type! We're like toothpaste and lemonade – we don't go together at all! And what about my boycott?

Charlie liked her. He didn't have to ask her to come back over the air – with the whole school listening. And he didn't have to do it by playing such a sweet song. Such an un-Charlie song. But maybe there was more to Charlie than Riley knew. Maybe he was deeper and more complicated than he seemed.

"Oh, no, Chloe," Riley gasped. "I like him, too! And I don't just *like* like him. I like him – like *that*!"

Chloe stared at her sister in shock. "You like Charlie? You *like* like him?" She shook her head and sighed. "Riley, you're in for it now."

chapter fourteen

"How did this happen?" Riley wailed. "I thought he was a jerk! And he thought he was so superior to me! When did it all switch around?"

Chloe shrugged. "These things happen, I guess."

Suddenly Riley couldn't wait to see him again. She finished dressing and she and Chloe hurried to school. She had to get there before the end of the morning show. She wanted to be on the *Rant* again.

The show had ten minutes left when she walked into the radio station. Charlie looked up from the soundboard. She gave him a little wave hello. He broke into a grin and waved her into the studio.

"Okay, kids, your prayers have been answered," Charlie said into the mike. "I've got a surprise for you."

Riley leaned into her mike and said, "Bad morning, West Malibu! I'm back!"

"You heard right," Charlie said. "Riley is back on *Morning Death Rant*! So, Riley, in honor of your return,

I'll let you pick a song to close out the show. What will it be, Riley?"

Riley reached into her bag for a CD she'd brought. "I want to play 'Sunny Day Feeling' by the Sugartones," she announced.

"What? To close out the *Death Rant*?" Charlie protested. "I'm sorry, Riley. I was willing to play some of the songs you liked so you'd come back. But the Sugartones? That's going too far."

"What are you saying, Charlie?" Riley said. "You want me to quit again?" She liked the song but not that much. Mostly she wanted to test Charlie. To see how far he'd go to get her back.

"No, no, please don't quit again," Charlie said. He took the CD from her and put it into the player. "All right, you win. Here's 'Sunny Day Feeling' to close us out. Now it truly *is* a bad morning."

He pressed play and winced at the sound of the bright, chirpy song. The show was over for the day.

"You came back," Charlie said after they'd left the studio. "My little plan worked."

"Plan? What plan?" Riley asked.

"It wasn't exactly complicated," Charlie admitted. "I just thought if I played some of the songs you like, you'd see that I can be flexible. When it's important to me, I mean."

Riley smiled. "So can I," she said.

"I'm really sorry about the mess I made for Chloe and Lennon," Charlie added. "I swear I didn't mean to play the wrong song. But then you quit, and I got all flustered, and I forgot all about Lennon's request. I didn't think of fixing it until today, when I remembered what a big mistake I'd made."

"That's okay," Riley said. "Chloe will understand." She paused. "I'm really glad you asked me to come back. I missed the show a lot."

"Just the show?" Charlie asked.

"Well, mostly," Riley said.

[Riley: If he thinks he's going to get me to admit I like him, he's crazy!]

"We should plan some of next week's shows," Charlie said. "Want to get together after school today?"

"Sure," Riley said. "Let's meet at California Dream."

"California Dream? That conformity factory?" Charlie protested. "What about the Aztec?"

The Aztec was a dingy punk coffeehouse. "The Aztec?" Riley said. "It's too dark in there. And too noisy."

She crossed her arms and stood her ground. He crossed his arms, too. They faced off. I won't give in, Riley thought.

Charlie let his arms fall to his sides. "All right," he said. "We can meet at California Dream this once. But we won't be making a habit of it."

The bell rang, and they headed for their homerooms. Riley sighed happily. The Riley and

Charlie Show was back! And, she guessed, her boycott was now officially over. It was a little pathetic – the boycott was supposed to have lasted three months! And she'd only stayed boy-free for a little over a week.

Oh, well, she thought. Who cares? I like Charlie, and Charlie likes me. And he's not like other guys – that's for sure.

"Did you hear the *Rant* this morning?" Lennon asked Chloe. He stopped her at her locker before lunch. She'd been looking for him all morning but hadn't seen him until now.

"I heard it," she said.

"So you're willing to talk to me again?" he asked. He looked nervous. "You'll listen to what I have to say? You won't run away?"

"I won't run away," Chloe promised. "I realize now that Charlie made a mistake, and you were only trying to do something nice for me, not insult me. But you can see how I'd misunderstand."

"Totally," Lennon said. "I wish I'd listened to the radio show after I made that dedication! But I didn't have my Walkman with me. I just assumed Charlie would get it right. I didn't know he played the wrong song until you dumped milk on my head!"

"But that still doesn't explain all the other bad things you did," Chloe said. "Like spilling coffee all over me at the Newsstand."

"That was an accident!" Lennon protested.

"Well, what about giving me a half-dead yellow rose?" Chloe asked. "Don't you know how bad it is if your boyfriend gives you a yellow rose?"

"No!" Lennon said. "I mean, I do now. But I didn't then. All I knew was that you liked the color yellow. So I thought you'd like a yellow rose. I didn't know it was a bad thing until I went back to the flower shop and told them you got upset about it. The florist explained the whole rose-color thing to me. Chloe, I'm sorry. I didn't mean it."

Chloe leaned back against her locker and thought about what Lennon was saying. He's been trying to communicate with me, she realized. That's what he's been doing all along. He's just not very good at it. Make that, he's very, very bad at it. Especially for such a smart guy.

"Chloe, I know I messed up," Lennon said. "But I'm trying to tell you something. Something that's hard for me to say."

"What is it?" she asked.

I'll give him one last chance, she thought, steeling herself against another disappointment. What was he going to say? What if it wasn't as good as she hoped? What if he let her down again?

"I – I can't seem to come right out and say it," he said. "But it's a good thing. I was just trying to find another way to let you know, without using the words. But everything kept going wrong, and then you wouldn't even listen to me!"

"So what are you trying to say?" she asked again. He was being a little wishy-washy, which worried her.

"What do you think?" he asked.

She looked at his face. With his big blue eyes he gazed at her like a lovesick puppy – the way Pepper did when Chloe brushed her.

He definitely likes me, she thought. But so what? He's my boyfriend – he's supposed to like me. But I told *him* I loved him. That's when all the trouble started.

Lennon pulled something out of his backpack. "Here," he said. "This is for you. I hope I got it right this time."

He presented her with a rose. A deep red rose.

"Red stands for love!" Chloe cried. She squinted at him suspiciously. "You knew that...didn't you?" she asked. She didn't want the meaning of the rose to be just another mistake.

"Yes, I knew it," Lennon said.

"Does that mean you love me?" she asked.

He nodded.

I guess that's good enough, Chloe thought. So he can't say the actual words yet. So what? He can nod yes. He loves me!

"That thing you said to me on Valentine's Day?" Lennon said. "I couldn't say it back but I was really glad you said it."

"Me, too," Chloe said. She glanced around to make sure nobody was watching, then she threw her arms around his neck and kissed him. He kissed her, too.

"So everything's cool again?" he asked.

She pulled back and looked around again. A couple walked by holding hands. Down the hall a girl laughed and tickled her boyfriend. Chloe spotted some pink and red paper hearts taped onto a bulletin board, left over from Valentine's Day.

"Everything's cool," she said. She sniffed the red rose. It smelled like love. Which made sense, since love was all over West Malibu High that day.

Love was in the air!

so little time

Check out book 14!

spring breakup

"Chloe! What're you doing?" Quinn demanded. Chloe was so startled she almost dropped her nail polish wand on the floor.

"What?" she asked.

"That's Miss Scarlet. You can't put Miss Scarlet on your toes when you just put Peaches and Cream on your fingers," Quinn said. "You're going to clash."

Chloe looked down at the streak of red nail polish across her big toenail. She hadn't even realized she'd picked up the bottle of Miss Scarlet.

Quinn, Tara and Amanda were all staring at her through green avocado facemasks that matched her own. Chloe sighed.

"I guess I was distracted staring at the clock," she said. She picked up a cotton ball and wiped her toenail clean. "Riley's going to miss curfew."

"I'm not surprised," Tara said, returning to her nail filing. "Charlie does not seem like the type who brings his dates home on time."

"I have bad feeling about this," Chloe said, choosing a cocoa color that coordinated better with the peach. "Does anyone else think Charlie is a little..."

"Lame?" Tara supplied for her.

"Yeah! I mean, he didn't get up off his butt once all day at the beach house," Chloe said.

"Does he think he's too good for Jonah Bayou?" Quinn put in.

"Maybe he's just not a good dancer or something," Amanda suggested.

"Okay, but then why come at all?" Chloe said. "He totally brought the place down. And I barely saw Riley all day. She couldn't possibly have had any fun."

At that moment the door to Riley and Chloe's bedroom opened and Riley walked in. She stared dreamily at the ceiling and almost put her foot in the bowl of avocado mask that was sitting on the floor.

"Riley! Stop!" Chloe shouted. She dove over and pulled the bowl out of the way.

Riley laughed. "Thanks, Chloe. I don't think my foot needs a facial."

Chloe glanced at her friends. Riley looked completely dazed.

"So, how was your date?" Chloe asked. Riley plopped down on her bed, bouncing up and down.

"It was *so* much fun," she said. "We went skateboarding and had ice cream and then Charlie's friends Frodo and Jessie showed up."

"Wait a minute, F*rodo*?" Chloe asked.

"Yeah. He was really funny. But you should see Jessie. He has this tattoo of a dragon that goes up his neck and onto his right cheek," Riley said. "It's so cool."

"You're kidding, right?" Chloe said. "A face tattoo?"

"I know. I was a little freaked at first, but he's nice once you get to know him. And funny," Riley said. "He and Frodo both work at Taco Hut every day."

"Isn't Taco Hut that place where all the freaks hang out?" Chloe said.

"Yeah. The one on the boardwalk that everyone walks by a little faster?" Amanda said.

"That's the place, but I bet it's not that bad," Riley said. "Jessie and Frodo eat there every day."

"Ew. I hope they didn't breathe on you," Quinn said.

"Seriously. That's a 911 for the people at Listerene," Tara put in.

Riley laughed. "Well, I thought they were cool. And Charlie and I had a very romantic night. He kissed me. Twice."

"Really?" Chloe said. "That's so great."

She grinned, happy for her sister who was clearly falling hard. But inside, she just did not get it. Skateboarding and ice cream? Chilling with Frodo and Mr. Face Tattoo? How was that romantic?

"So, are you coming to the beach house on Monday?" Chloe asked as Riley started to get ready for bed. Normally she would have assumed Riley would be there, but with Charlie in the picture, Chloe wasn't so sure. Maybe she'd spend the day chowing down on Mondo Tacos with the skater-boys.

"Wouldn't miss it," Riley said.

"Is Charlie coming?" Quinn asked.

Chloe held her breath.

"No. He has to work," Riley said.

"Oh. That's too bad," Chloe said.

Inside, she was actually kind of excited that Charlie wouldn't be joining them again. He clearly hadn't had fun and Riley clearly had less fun with him there. Now at least Chloe would get to hang out with her sister all day and Riley would get to enjoy the beach house.

It was the best thing for everybody...right?

mary-kateandashley

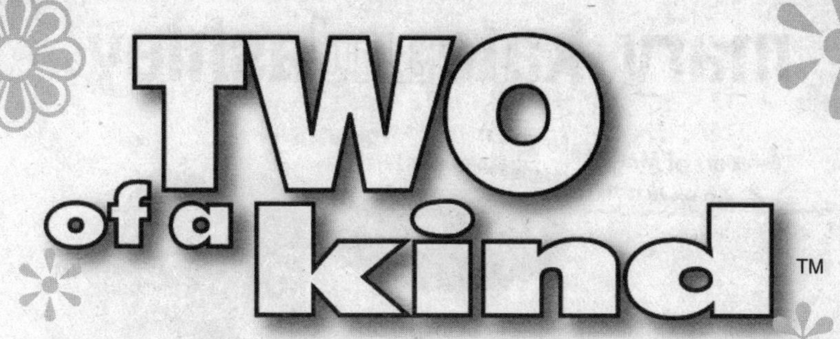

(16)	Likes Me, Likes Me Not	(0 00 714465 2)
(17)	Shore Thing	(0 00 714464 4)
(18)	Two for the Road	(0 00 714463 6)
(19)	Surprise, Surprise!	(0 00 714462 8)
(20)	Sealed with a Kiss	(0 00 714461 X)
(21)	Now you see him, Now you don't	(0 00 714446 6)
(22)	April Fool's Rules	(0 00 714460 1)
(23)	Island Girls	(0 00 714445 8)
(24)	Surf Sand and Secrets	(0 00 714459 8)
(25)	Closer Than Ever	(0 00 715881 5)
(26)	The Perfect Gift	(0 00 715882 3)
(27)	The Facts About Flirting	(0 00 715883 1)
(28)	The Dream Date Debate	(0 00 715854 X)
(29)	Love-Set-Match	(0 00 715885 8)
(30)	Making a Splash	(0 00 715886 6)

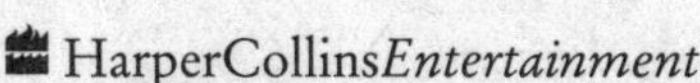

MARY-KATE OLSEN ASHLEY OLSEN

BIG FUN IN THE BIG APPLE!

MARY-KATE OLSEN AND ASHLEY OLSEN IN THE BIG SCREEN HIT

PACKSHOT ARTWORK SUBJECT TO CHANGE